MERE

Esta Spalding & Linda Spalding

MERE

HarperPerennialCanada
HarperCollinsPublishersLtd

Mere

For information address:
HarperCollins Publishers Ltd.,
55 Avenue Road, Suite 2900,
Toronto, Ontario, Canada M5R 3L2

www.harpercanada.com

HarperCollins books may be purchased for educational, business, or sales promotional use.
For information please write:
Special Markets Department,
HarperCollins Canada,
55 Avenue Road, Suite 2900,
Toronto, Ontario, Canada M5R 3L2

First HarperPerennial Canada edition

National Library of Canada Cataloguing in Publication

Spalding, Esta
Mere / Esta Spalding & Linda Spalding.

ISBN 0-00-648523-5

I. Spalding, Linda II. Title.

PS8587.P214M47 2002 C813'.54
C2002-902411-0
PR9199.3.S613M47 2002

RRD 9 8 7 6 5 4 3 2 1

Printed and bound in the United States
Set in Monotype Plantin

I will not let thee go,
except thou bless me.

Genesis 32:26

PROLOGUE

They sailed out of the mouth of the Niagara River on the last day of October, when the great lake seemed gradually to change shape, becoming shallower, reflecting less sky, as if the work of the summer—holding the great overriding sun in its cup—was done. It was the time when Faye and her crew—two children on a steel-hulled ship—sailed into Toronto for one of their twice-yearly visits, when Mark, who was sixteen, and Mere, who was twelve, began anticipating the event days in advance. They were planning a joint attack on the city—food, yes, and supplies, but also cigarettes, gum, a fresh hoard of magazines.

"How much longer?" Mere asked her mother.

Standing at the helm, Faye was taut as strained rope. Hard life on the *Persephone*, lived fully in wind and rain and even snow, had eroded all but the necessary muscle and bone. Even her voice was harsh. "You figure it out. How many miles across is the lake at this point?"

Mere turned to Mark. "How many?"

Mark had already measured the distance on the chart.

"Twenty-four miles." He sounded laconic. "We'll get there this afternoon if the wind stays up and southerly."

Faye looked at Mere. "It's going to swing north."

Mere's hopes were more dependent on weather than her mother suspected, because this time, as they came into Toronto, her father might appear on the dock and salute her with the fastidious charm she'd attached to her fragile memory of him. Faye always told her that he was gone for good. "There's no point looking for him in every port. It wasn't like that with us." But it was only a matter of time, Mere believed. After all, someone gave the dock master in Toronto an envelope full of cash twice a year. Who would leave it, if not her father? Last April, Mere had left a letter, slipping it into the dock master's hand. *Holmes,* she'd written on the envelope. Her last name. She'd written that they'd be back in October. *Do you live in a skyscraper? If you do, then you can watch for us.* She had been about to describe the boat—fifty-six feet long, with a square sail on the forward mast and a rectangular sail aft—but then she'd thought how stupid that would be since he had once lived on the boat. Did he know they'd painted the hull blue? *If you see us, please come down to the dock to say hello.* She had almost written *to meet me,* but that was stupid too, so she had signed the note *Mere* and left it at that.

Now, standing beside her mother, she decided she wanted to be alone to savor the sweet anticipation of sailing into the city.

"Don't go too far. If the wind swings around, I'll need you on deck." Faye watched the water shudder away from the hull, its subtle changes in opacity more familiar to her

than any other home. *Where are we?* she thought. I
Thirteen years of this. She had not intended to live he
as a fugitive on a piece of steel. But here, out of sight of land, the three of them were safe. If there were a way to stay in the middle of the lake and never go to shore, she would have found it by now. But the envelope of cash was a necessity. *Necessity*, she thought, *a clever mother.*

And her child? Except for the brutal winters when they docked but lived on the boat, Mere had never known land-life. Spared the complications of human society, she was like one of those children found in the forest, uncomprehending and uncivilized. A lucky or unlucky child.

Mere lay on her stomach in the wide netting under the bowsprit, hanging her hands down through the knotted ropes and dragging them in the rushing water. To Mark, who lay beside her, the layer of air around her hands underwater looked like filmy gloves. The light off the water was blue and green, and the wind was warm with the last breath of Indian summer. "Swim?" Mere said, throwing her legs over the bowsprit so that she sat on it like a hobby horse. The bow of the boat pointed at Toronto, a compass needle.

They shimmied the bowsprit and slipped onto the deck. "Faaaye!" Mere's voice was carried by wind. "Faaaye, we're going to swim!"

Faye pointed up at the square sails. They would have to douse them to slow the boat. Mark was already letting go of the lines that held the sails taut. He headed up one side of the mast on the ladder of ropes and Mere headed up the other. Then, stepping off the ratlines and onto the long cable strung from yardarm to yardarm, they leaned over and heaved the sail up, like heaps of heavy laundry.

Back on deck, Mark unlaced his boots and Mere stripped down to her underwear.

Mere waited for the movement of the boat to lull her into thinking that she wasn't going to jump—the lake would be too cold—and then she hurled herself at the water, taking a long, hard breath and letting it out as she hit.

The cold was terrible, but Mere would not scream. She turned over on her back and watched the huge hull slide past, blocking out everything. This was how they measured the speed of the boat—by dropping a wooden block off the bowsprit and counting the seconds till it passed the stern. One-enchilada, two-enchilada, three—now she could see the brass letters on the hull moving away, getting tinier, like Faye's face. Faye, smiling and waving. Then the smile disappeared, the eyes and nose vanished. Her mother was just a shape. Mere felt for the rope in the water . . . What if she didn't hold on? What if the rope slipped away, the letters on the hull disappeared, Faye's face turned into a smudge without features . . . and the lake was all her own for as long as she could swim? How long? She took the rope in her hands and felt it drag her forward. Mark surfaced beside her.

His toughness and muscles made Mere aware of herself. He took hold of the rope, letting his legs float up by her shoulders. He was not much taller than she was, but his feet, his hands, his laugh were bolder. Mere let go of the rope, then grabbed on again. Let go, grabbed on. She kept her head underwater, hearing the lake roar in her ears like a mob, seeing, for a minute, Mark's dark eyes and face, his slightly crooked teeth. The sound of the lake was enormous.

Now her hands let go of the rope. She pulled her head out of the water and watched for a split second as the boat moved away, cutting the dark water evenly. For that split second, she felt the suck of gravity from the lake bottom far below, demanding and magnetic. *Man overboard*, she thought secretly, because it was a phrase Faye never allowed them to say, never even to think—unless it was true. The expanse of water between her and the boat . . . If she didn't hold on to the rope, it would be true. *Man overboard.* They had not passed another boat all day. She was inside the lake now, opening her eyes underneath and seeing nothing except white hands at the ends of arms propelling her forward as they felt for the lifeline. There. Its prickly slime. Had anyone noticed that she'd slipped away? She felt Mark beside her, wishing for a second that he had noticed, then wishing that her mother had, because it was exciting to be lost for even a moment.

Faye had been watching. Seeing Mere surface too far behind the boat, she'd clutched at the rail and stopped herself from shouting at her daughter.

Mark put his arms around Mere. They were touching, bare against bare. Then he yelled up, "Hey, old lady! Ain't it your turn?" It was the way he teased Faye—the reference to age, the bad grammar. "Hey! Come in!"

"Okay, big stuff, come steer."

As he toweled himself off at the helm, Faye appeared wearing four shirts and a pair of jeans, holding a bottle of the detergent they used to wash everything—dishes, clothes, the decks, their hair—because Faye said soap was soap. She hoisted herself up to the deckhouse and launched herself into the air, pulling her legs in to her body and wrapping her arms around them to make a cannonball. Then she swam back to the boat, yanking herself through the churning water against the drag of dirty clothes.

Mere was hanging off the rope near the stern. "Soap," she called up to Mark.

Watching from above, Mark felt a sharp pang of protectiveness. Mere was lathering her hair, scrubbing her fingernails into her scalp. Like a raccoon, he thought, or an otter. Like an animal without a single guilty thought.

Faye was scrubbing the clothes on her body, rolling herself in the water like the agitator on a washing machine. With one arm, she clung to the line while she reached for Mark with the other, making him pull her up to the deck. It wasn't hard. Faye was small-boned and light on her feet, in spite of the ferocity with which she ran the boat and their lives. At thirty-three, she was already starting to look old, and in the bright sunlight, he saw that her hair was going gray. Too much worry, Mark thought. She worries for Mere, who is her child, and for me, who is not.

Mere watched the slow stream of suds that trailed behind the boat like the white brush stroke of an airplane in the sky. She looked up at Mark, who was concentrating on the compass, and at her mother standing beside him, shaking out her hair. She was glad to be the last to get out, to get warm. They were only a few hours from Toronto, where her father might be waiting.

A DOG

The late afternoon light was fading as they neared the city, and warmth turned to winter chill. Each of them felt the snap of wind, a sudden drop in temperature. Their wet hair, icy in the north wind. It was the change in the weather Faye had predicted. A pale line of masts bobbed in the harbor—sails already folded into sail bags for the winter—and behind the spectral masts gray lake bled into gray sky, gray freighters, gray grain elevators. Mere went below for her windbreaker.

Faye pointed the bow of the ship toward the harbor entrance and chewed on a finger distractedly. Behind the laundry drying on the rigging, she could see the city that glittered in the setting light. Bank towers, the white sugar refinery, the raised expressway. Wicked illusions. "Douse the sails."

"We're motoring in?"

"Correct."

"But we have to set the sails," Mere complained. "It

looks so much better." She was imagining a man somewhere in one of those buildings, lifting binoculars to his eyes and scanning the harbor for the *Persephone*'s sails.

"I don't care what it looks like." Faye planned to be in and out of the city quickly before anyone had really noticed they were there. Thinking this, she added, "Mark, be quick with the supplies, and no shore leave, Mere."

"Mark needs me to help!" Mere used the wind as her excuse to shout. It was better than whining, which her mother despised. "And I'm old enough!"

Once the sails were doused and bagged, Mere slouched against the rigging in her jeans and windbreaker, glaring at the chicken coops lashed to the deckhouse and fighting an impulse to argue.

"Be with me on this, Mere."

"I'm not with you." She skulked along the deck toward the bow, looking up at the CN tower that loomed over the shoreline like one hand of a vanished clock. All day they'd watched it grow on the horizon.

Now Faye reversed the engines, and Mark launched himself at the dock, landing with a *thud* and throwing the line in his hand over the black bollard bolted there. He ran up the pier toward the bow, and Mere heaved a thick line at his shoulders. Then she kneeled, pulling in the slack rope as the boat inched closer. No one spoke; the three of them had been docking the *Persephone* in just this way since the day Mark had first appeared seven years before. When the ship was firmly alongside and all lines were made fast, Mark set off toward the city with Faye's list of supplies in his pocket, and Faye moved into the deckhouse to fill out the log. Mere was left alone on deck to check her rage. *I'm not with you.*

She swung her legs over the railing and pulled herself up the ratlines, counting the buildings along the skyline, the two matching black towers that faced each other, the sprawling stone hotel with its green roofs, and a new skyscraper of golden glass. When she looked down at the land, she saw a man coming toward the boat carrying a large dog in his arms and wearing a pack on his back. The head of the dog was hanging down like something dead. The man yelled up, "Liza! Liza!" Saying it twice.

"No one here by that name," Mere shouted down at him, shaking her head, but when he continued his progress toward her, she wrapped her legs around the metal stay, positioned her sneakers on the wire, and slid down to the deck. A stranger to sailing life would have been surprised by this maneuver, but the man smiled and stepped across the gangway, striding onto deck and causing the boat to rock.

"I brought my dog," he said to Mere in a soft voice, adjusting the animal in his arms. He spoke as if Mere should know what he meant, as if she'd long ago invited him to a party, and he'd only now arrived with some crucial ingredient.

Before Mere could answer, she saw her mother come out of the deckhouse, put a hand over her dark eyes, and look off through the hard-setting light. The shadow on her cheekbones gave the impression of a mask.

"The thing about dogs is that you can hang onto them," the man said, glancing at the chicken coops.

Faye didn't look at him.

Mere had puzzled over the events of her childhood so many times that she had forgotten what was real and what was made up. But even so, looking at this man with the dog in his arms, she knew she'd expected someone different and tested her imagined father against the real man in front of her. This one had no beard. He had gray eyes.

Like mine, Mere thought.

Faye set down the can of gasoline she was carrying. When she spoke, her voice caught. "Why now—?"

The dog twitched, but the man held onto him, and just for an instant Mere knew why they had never lived on the land—but then she quickly forgot. She tried to swallow, though her mouth felt like sand. She wanted her mother to see that she was ready for whatever was going to happen, ready for her father. She said, "Can he do any tricks?"

"We have to get going," Faye announced.

The man set the dog down next to Mere's feet, saying, "He can pray," and with that the dog lay down, crossed his paws, and put his nose between them.

"Off the boat." Faye pointed at the man.

But he stretched out both hands. "Merril. And you're Mere."

She hesitated, recognizing that his name was almost hers, then looked at her mother, who had put both her hands on her hips. Unsmiling.

"What do you think of your old man?" he asked.

Heart leaping in her chest, Mere stood absolutely erect.

It was her father who broke the silence. "That's a hazard there," he said, walking toward Faye and picking up the gasoline can. Mere stared at the can. The man was right, and Mere understood that her father made her mother careless.

"Why now?" Faye said again.

"Trouble," Merril said, and what Mere heard next was "I have to come back with you."

"Take the dog for a walk, Mere. Do it now."

"I thought you said no shore leave."

"Right now. Up and down the quay. Stay close by."

The dog resisted following Mere across the small gap between boat and dock, but she tugged on his collar, furious with her mother, who knew exactly how to ruin everything. "Come." She spoke to the dog. "You're supposed to follow. You have to mind me."

Her father had come to find her, and suddenly Mere felt alone in a certain way, and because she was thinking about this, she did not think about the fear she had seen in her mother's face. She thought about the years her father had been living apart from them, years she might have known him. "My trouble with your father has nothing to do with you," Faye always said. But Mere knew that wasn't true. It had everything to do with her because it kept him away from her.

Hanging on to the dog, Mere moved up the quay and into an alley formed by two of the grain elevators, an alley dusty from the wind and dark because the sun had all but disappeared, an alley thick with the bitter smell of hops. Mere stood, her eyes half closed. *On the boat, I can never get away from her.*

The boat was more like a body than anything else, and Mere knew every breath of it, every smell and every seam, every mood and every flaw. The way she knew her mother. The way she knew Mark. The way she knew exactly the drift of diesel that came when the wind was down and that used to make the boys they hid under the bunks feel sleepy and sick.

In the past few months, Mere had been thinking things she could never tell her mother. These thoughts had made her secretive and short-tempered, but most of all, ashamed. When had she last lain on Faye's bunk being read to or having her hair brushed and braided? When had they last eaten caramels two at a time, trying to outlast each other at savoring, pretending to have swallowed and then displaying the small bit of sweetness left on the tongue?

From her hiding place behind the grain elevator Mere watched her mother's gestures, trying to read their meaning.

When Merril edged closer to Faye, she turned away from his gaze. Her response to panic was a rigid coldness. "What happened?"

Swinging the pack off his shoulders, he said, "I have to go with you until I can get to a safe place. Yesterday there was clicking on my phone line. And last night a van in the alley outside my house. This morning I found Marlboro butts in the driveway."

"Meaning?" She had noticed the changes in him. Now she began to see the familiar things. His hands were still rough and calloused, his hair still dark, his face wide, the skin stretched tight over his cheekbones. For years, she had wondered how they would meet again.

"They're American." He winced.

"FBI." At that moment, a seagull landed on the rail, a

man walked past, somewhere a siren released its cry into the air. Faye's instinct was to grab Merril's arm and pull him below, where they could talk without being seen. What if they had followed him to the boat? "They haven't picked you up." She said it slowly, her voice brittle.

He looked away from her and then back. "I haven't asked anything of you. I haven't bothered you for something like ten or eleven years."

"Nine and a half."

Merril glanced around, gestured at the rigging, the deck. "It's been hard to keep the boat going by yourself. I can see that. That's another reason I came down. Because admit it, you could use some help." His eyes came back to her.

Faye remembered a time when his hands and arms had been important to her, when she had been able to stand still and watch this man take over lines, helm, sails, and a petulant engine. *Ahab! Liza! Steel yourselves!* "This is my boat," she gasped. It was impossible to give an inch. "Now get off."

Merril refused to budge. "Congratulations on becoming as shitty and selfish and venal as the rest of the world."

She had never seen him this frightened. But she would not be swayed. She would have to take Mere and Mark off the boat this instant. No disguise would be good enough. Faye pulled at his shirt. "Please. Go away. Let me take care of our child."

Faye was waiting for him to get angry, to ridicule her or bully her, to follow the old path of their lost and futile arguments.

But Merril didn't argue. Instead he turned his back to her, looking out at the darkening city.

From behind the great mass of concrete, Mere watched closely as Merril moved away and Faye cupped her hands around her mouth to call out, "Mere. Mere?"

Heart beating wildly, Mere clutched at the dog, one hand in his fur, the other around his collar. Her father was being sent away, and now Faye would not even give her a few minutes with him. Merril stepped off the boat and walked toward the grain elevators without looking back. He was slouched over from the heaviness of his pack and appeared to be defeated by the small woman standing firm on the deck of her boat. His hair was long enough to be blown about his face. When he turned the corner of the path between the towers, Mere stepped out and looked up at him. She saw that his face was pale. "I forgot to ask his name," she said about the dog, sounding bolder than she felt. She continued staring, never having learned to look away from a face.

Merril said, "I call him Rogue because I found him in the ravine."

The dog was glad to see him, and when Mere loosened her grip, he rushed at the man and barked.

"Quiet!" Merril commanded, looking around warily.

Her father stood firmly before her, not dream, but flesh. On the other side of the tower, her mother might still be shouting. Mere tried not to think of this. "I like Rogue. Where does he live?" Then she stopped herself, wishing she had undone her braid. "I'm almost thirteen," she said, tucking it under the collar of her windbreaker and adding, "You never looked for us." Then, "Did you get my note?"

Merril didn't answer. Instead, he picked up Rogue as if he intended to take the dog away again, as if Mere had said something unforgiving and wrong.

"I keep your clock in a secret place," she told him, and he looked at her as she had hoped he would do, stopping in his tracks.

"Clock?"

Mere sighed. "It was in a bag I found full of stuff. I remember you showed it to me when I was little."

A sudden laugh. "Oh, the . . . well, I'm glad you took care of it. Is my stuff still on the boat?"

Mere nodded. She had an impulse to run back and open her locker where she kept the clock. It would be something she could offer him. But Merril began to walk through the dust and gravel. He walked in a hurry, looking over his shoulder, and she decided that he must be checking to see if she was following. *Up and down the quay. Stay close.* Her mother's instructions, but Mere couldn't worry about them now. She trailed after her father.

As they came out at the northern end of the alley, she caught up with him, noticing his nervousness. They were alone together at last. She tried smiling. "Actually, I'm very excellent with non-human beings. I could train Rogue," she said, to put her father at ease, and to show her usefulness. They passed the garbled construction sites around the edge of the harbor, where everything was changing shape. He put his hand on her hair. The hand was heavy, pressing down, and Mere wanted to tell him to take it back, but she did not.

Faye crouched by the helm and pulled her knees up to her chest, trying to breathe deeply, trying to remember her old prescriptions for staying calm. A phrase came to her: fight or flight. But there was only one option.

They had decided that morning to anchor for the night across the harbor in Lighthouse Cove. She knew the cove was a place Mere and Mark looked forward to. Alone or together, they'd go off to the marsh where they could smoke cigarettes, something Faye had forbidden on the boat. But now they couldn't go to the cove, now they must leave, anything but stay here at the foot of the city, waiting, the mast swinging like a pendulum counting the hours. Had Merril been followed?

She wanted a cigarette. Below deck, she took a canvas bag from the cabinet under her bunk. Nothing. Not even a stub. Smoking might cause the sails to catch fire. *Let them burn*, she thought. Burn the boat down, destroy any trace—*there is more than enough dynamite*—but first let her have Mark and Mere.

Mark. He must have a few cigarettes in his locker, even at the end of a long stretch like the past few weeks. She moved quickly to the forward cabin where he slept, and opened the locker, taking in its harsh smell, fumbling through sneakers, paperbacks, playing cards, slamming it shut again. Mere's locker was neater than Mark's, but not by much. Her diary sat on top of a pile of clothes, a long string taped to it, a pencil taped to the end of the string so Mere could sit up in the rigging and write—there were so many ways they'd lashed themselves down. Never in all these years had Faye gone through her daughter's heart. Privacy was a rule, and a convenient one for all of them.

Forgetting the cigarette, Faye slammed the second door shut and navigated the long corridor almost drunkenly, past the engine room to the galley.

Who could she ask for help? Gil. Wherever he was—in a house or an apartment, in an office in Toronto. Over the years, she had thought of him only vaguely. Did she have the right to ask for his help?

In the galley, cups and plates had been carefully stowed, but Faye picked up a sponge and scrubbed at the stove. *Mere. Come back now.* She scrubbed the kettle, a piece of her history. *Leave things clean.* Then filled it at the faucet, pumping the water with her foot, and set it to boil. *Use up the fuel.* Mere must be stalling. Merril would have found her with the dog and tried to extricate himself. "She's trying to teach me a lesson," Faye said aloud, remembering that Mere had done this before after an argument about shore leave. Perhaps even now Mere was with Mark. With that, Faye climbed the ladder up to the deck, emerging into the artificial light of the city and moving to the chicken coops as if walking through deep water, opening the fragile wire gates that were carefully clipped shut. *Blow up the statue! It'll be prophetic!* Without speaking to the chickens she had tended and raised, she pulled them out, one after the other, scattering them across the deck.

Mere followed Merril along the sidewalk and tried to think of what she should say. All these years spent waiting. All these years practicing to be interesting enough for a father. She should be talking about the dog, but a picture of her mother's hairbrushes kept coming into her head. There were three of them, and they lay on top of the small oak counter in Faye's cabin. From the beginning of memory, Mere had known that she was special because she was allowed to go in and out of Faye's cabin as no one else was, not the boys they carried to Canada, and later, not even Mark. She would knock on the low door, then push on into the cabin's particular weather, a dense smell of diesel, lake water, and cedar. The hairbrushes lay with their bristles exposed, like animals, stomach-up. One was harder and the bristles were farther apart. Another was softer with closer bristles. The last was so soft and the bristles so close that pushing it through her hair was work. Mere would sit down on the bunk that took up most of the space in the cabin and look out the porthole as Faye brushed her hair, beginning with the hardest bristles and finishing with the softest. Here was comfort, just as when Faye said, "You're with me forever," knowing there was no other place Mere could be. Or sometimes, when Mere had learned a particularly hard lesson, Faye would say, "Accepting consequences is harder than anything."

In this way, Faye organized Mere's world, although the clarity of that world made Mere want to push against it. Once, Mere had sneaked off the boat and gone for shore leave, returning with stolen gum in her mouth. Faye had pulled her by the arm down into her cabin and pointed to the hairbrushes, forcing Mere to choose the one that fit her wrong action. Mere had chosen the hardest one, wanting her mother to know that her pleasure had been worth it, that no spanking was going to scare her.

What would Faye do this time?

It would be wrong to tell her father about the hairbrushes. Besides, he probably already knew about them, if he had lived with her mother—a thought that, in itself, was extraordinary. She looked at him again, registering that he had lived with her mother, eaten and worked and slept there with both of them long before Mark ever came. Vaguely she remembered a time when the boat was maneuvering a lock. It was a memory she had nurtured and embellished, a vision of her father. He held the long ropes that tied them to the dock. Faye stood at the helm, and the water jets started with a fierce roaring. The boat dropped, and the walls of the lock grew tall beside them, while Mere held on to her mother's legs. The walls rose up and up, dwarfing the *Persephone*'s mast and making Mere afraid. It was her father who shouted to her that they were all right. She could see him at the bow working his rope, his mouth open in a laugh that she could not hear over the thunder of man-made weather.

Now he held the dog in his arms and showed no sign of weariness, as if he'd been carrying one thing or another all his life. They were passing the old terminal building, a large concrete warehouse, and Mere pointed to its roof, blurting out, "I've been up there. We had a fight with fire extinguishers. Faye found out. I think Mark told her. He's different from me because he wants her to know things. But I have my own life." It was too much to tell at once, and she immediately regretted what she'd said.

"They're going to make a mall there, in that building, so people will come down here to the waterfront to shop." He seemed to be talking to another grown-up. He set the dog down and walked on. "Clothes, jewelry . . ." He paused, perhaps searching for something to hold her interest or thinking about something else altogether. "Restaurants, movies. This city is full of things you've never even dreamed about."

The dog ambled along. Why had Merril ever carried him? Mere glanced at her father hopefully, then pointed, aiming her right arm north. "The building with the gold windows. What's it for?"

Merril stopped and gazed at the building, which seemed to send off its own radiant heat. He studied her. "You bored out there on the water? Freezing in the winter, boiling in the summer, and never meeting other kids?" His eyes swept up and down the street, squinting at a car that slowed down as it turned the corner.

"I don't have to live with Faye," Mere said, although it was a disloyalty that would later haunt her. Merril had not asked her why she was following him. *I've never spent a night without her*, she thought. There were those nights, anchored off one of the islands in the St. Lawrence River, when she and Mark had lowered the rowboat and gone to the island to camp in the woods, sleeping on the cushions from their bunks. They'd built a small fire and sat up late telling the scariest stories they could think of. But this, being with someone without telling her mother, was entirely different. She said, "Rogue likes me. Maybe I should see where he lives."

A taxi lurched past, spraying muddy water up around them, and Merril leapt after it, raising his hand, leaning into the window. "You take dogs?"

"She blind?" The driver pointed at Mere.

Merril nodded and opened the door.

"Fancy," Mere said, pointing to the taxi as if it were a limousine.

"You can't see it," Merril whispered. "You're blind."

She bobbed her head *yes*, thrilled that they were conspirators.

Taking her arm, he gave her a light shove, guiding her into the taxi. With her eyes closed, she could feel Rogue on the seat next to her, and tried to shove him over. She'd never been in a car before, but she did not tell Merril this. He threw his backpack into the trunk, then got into the taxi himself. "Cluny Drive," he said. "Take Rosedale Valley, okay?" Now he turned around completely, looking out the back window, and Mere almost turned to look herself, until she remembered that she was blind and closed her eyes.

He reached across her and locked her door. Mere felt the faint rumbling of the engine, and knew that being in a car was like being on a boat. It was perfectly safe. The four of them drove north away from the lake, and because any silence between them might cause him to reconsider her presence in the car, she said, "Anyway, like I said, I'm good with animals. I train chickens."

Merril leaned over to check on something in his back pocket. "Sure," he said, as if he'd known this all along, as if he had sworn on some parental Bible long ago to take her seriously when she spoke to him.

"Also," Mere announced, "I don't eat meat—"

"Like your mother," Merril commented.

Mere opened her eyes slightly, noticing now that his

face was not lined in the way her mother's was. She reached beside her, touching the dog, and said, "We're going to live on a farm, Mark and me."

"Who's this Mark?"

"I told you. He's my brother."

"I think I'd know if you had a brother," he said.

He was right. She'd have to be clearer now that she was talking to her father. "He's sort of my brother." Mere got quiet. She noticed Merril doing something with his mouth, pursing it. She kept facing him and not looking around. She had forgotten her blindness; her eyes were locked onto his, as if she had no real interest in the city, as if it was only a place of theory and possibility.

"You should see the city tonight," he said. "There's wind swirling leaves in the street, old newspapers . . . It's blustery out. And gray."

She closed her eyes again, then opened one of them a crack, wanting to ask him why he'd called her mother Liza. They turned west on a road where the trees were changing color and the headlights pulled out deep maroons.

"Pretty," he said, and the girl at his side said again, "Weird that you never even visited," finally turning away from him. Then she added, "It's not as if a boat's that hard to find."

It had begun to darken, and more wintry wind came up off the lake. When Faye at last saw Mark pushing a shopping cart down the long concrete dock, she leapt off the boat and rushed to him. "You took too long! Where's Mere?"

"You wouldn't let her go with me."

"Did you get the envelope?"

Mark reached into the pocket of his denim jacket and handed it over. "Something happened."

It wasn't a question, and Faye noticed the look on his face, but she ignored it, tearing the edge off the envelope and folding a thick stack of bills into her jeans pocket.

"Who was it?" Mark said. "Should I take off?"

"It wasn't about you."

"The fucking birds are out!" Mark moved to the gangway, dark eyes flashing.

"Watch your mouth. And get moving. Come on. Food on board and shove off." Faye grabbed a bag from the cart.

"Mere?"

"Must have gone to Lighthouse Cove." It was her last hope—that Mere had got on the ferry and gone to the cove on her own. After all, they'd had a fight. Maybe Mere just wanted to make a point. She would trick Faye into worrying and then make light of it, having no idea that Faye's worries were of an entirely different kind.

Loosening the lines from the dock, Mark noticed footprints in the gravel. A man's footprints, and a few that looked like Mere's. Also the paw prints of a dog.

It took only ten minutes to cross the harbor and enter the narrow lagoon, where Faye cut the engine and coasted in. She nosed the bow into the marsh under the arms of the willows, now leafless. Mark uncoiled longer lines and ran them through the forward rail, securing the boat to a couple of thick trees on shore. "Fucking chickens," Mark said, kicking one of them out of his way. Faye ducked into the deckhouse.

Once all lines were coiled and hung on their particular cleats, Mark hopped off the bowsprit, a lighted cigarette in his fingers, putting some distance between himself and Faye. He headed into tall grass that was already shocked stiff with frost. Faye stared for a moment at the ship's log. *Do you want to stop the war?* Her hands were trembling. She made no note of the day's events.

Mark sat in the tall grass smoking his cigarette. He was not the type to explore a person's reasons for doing things, but these were extraordinary circumstances, so he tried to reason through what he knew about Faye. She wasn't careless. But she was acting that way, leaving the dock without being certain where Mere was: that was something he'd never expected from her. And the chickens. There'd been someone, a man, around the boat. *It wasn't about you.* She wouldn't lie. So did this man have something to do with why she never left the boat for even a few minutes, why she practically held her breath every time they came into a harbor?

Now she sat upright on one of the benches around the helm. She would not lean back, but held herself against the night, waiting for Mere, watching the moon slash its course across the sky and the smoke from his cigarette curl up from the brittle grass. She must be crazy with worry, Mark thought, because she was more than crazy with love for Mere. Yet Faye was definitely hard on her daughter. He remembered the time she made Mere swim around the boat. He couldn't even recall what Mere had done, but he remembered the punishment: Faye walking around the deck holding on to the rope as if Mere were a dog.

Parents were supposed to do this, supposed to teach you about consequences. That's what he always told himself. He remembered going to the ocean with his parents. Curled in the back seat with his little brother, watching the wind in their mother's hair, the flush on their father's neck.

The drive to New Brunswick took hours. They stopped in Quebec at a campsite on a river across from a nuclear plant. Their father got out to pitch the tent. "Get me the stakes," he said. There were camper vans all around them strung with colored lights; people sat in folding chairs around barbecues, drinking beer, speaking what must have been French. After the tent was pitched, Mark and his brother left their father, wandering off to stand at the edge of one of the groups. People were passing jars of boiled eggs. They were frying fish. Mark and his brother watched them for a long time. It got dark. They couldn't find their way back to their own campsite. And when they did, much later, their father said that if they had missed dinner, well, then, they had missed dinner, and they'd probably want to miss the beach too. The next morning, he turned around and drove them home. The campsite had been only an hour away from the beach, so close, Mark remembered, he could smell the salt air. But he had still never seen the ocean.

He tried to tell Mere that Faye was just loving her when she gave her rules, but Mere couldn't understand that yet. She and her mother were more alike than they knew. That was it. They had to control everything, which was maybe why the land was all wrong for them. It was too wild, too unexpected, too wide.

He pulled another cigarette from the pack, lit it off the tail end of the last one. He'd keep smoking, one after another, just like that—it would pass the time until Mere came back. And Faye. He looked up at her, as she stood completely still, like one of those stone statues in a museum. A mother barely glancing at the baby she's nursing, staring back at the watcher with tired, glazed eyes—the pupils little hollowed-out circles in marble.

THE CLOCK

Faye always told the story of their lives in the manner of a ship's log. In this way, the fate of mother and daughter was the result of wind and weather, which wasn't entirely untrue. But there was more to the story, as there is more to a boat than wood, sail, and crew. When Mere was an infant, she could not be left alone on deck, and with so many risks below (grease, diesel, sewage, rust, peeling paint), Faye carried her daughter everywhere. Most of the time she wore Mere on her back, moving her around to the front when she replaced the ratlines that formed a ladder up the rigging, sometimes singing to keep the baby quiet. *We all live on a blue brigantine* . . . a useful lullaby.

According to the story, Mere's first steps had sent her lurching into the sail bags Faye had positioned in front of the sharp-edged bunks and cabinets in the main cabin. The motion of the ship was too much to combat, and for a time, Faye was afraid she would have to set up a permanent docking so that Mere could learn to walk. But eventually Mere walked in spite of the lake, gaining the confidence to hold the edges of benches and bunks and to take steps along the slippery deck. She adjusted her legs to the different kinds of rocking and swaying that took place under them, and was confused, after weeks of sailing, by an afternoon in port. Those were the hours of Faye's greatest worry. "I worry for the boys," was what she told Mere. Those were the hours of finding friendly authorities, of making the right contacts, and finally of giving her changelings to the Canadian shore.

As a growing child, Mere was strapped to Faye's view of the universe: the worry that one of the boys might get caught under the bunks halfway to Canada, the news on the radio of the war. Through it all, during those early years, Faye and Mere watched each other while Faye was in the deckhouse charting their course or on deck setting, folding, bagging the sails. In spite of the radio, and the boys, and the war, Mere sensed that her mother had abandoned the larger world, the world the boys disappeared into when they stepped off the boat.

Mere remembered a few of the boys, although the last one had left seven years before. The war was winding down, so he'd stayed on the boat for a long time, unable to decide whether to cast his lot with Canada or go back home. His draft number hadn't come up, so he might be safe. But once it did, if it did, escaping from the United States would be much harder. Faye had explained this to him and showed him a book called *How to Stay Out of the Army* that was stowed in the chart table. When he finally did jump off the boat in Kingston, Ontario, five-year-old Mere watched him walk away.

Her memories of her father were colored by the stories

she had told herself. He'd taught her the song about a drunken sailor. He'd put rum in the maple syrup and a fish under Faye's pillow. He used to lift Mere onto his shoulders and walk her up and down the deck while she touched lines and sails that were otherwise too high for her to reach. He taught her how to hold her fork. He bounced her on his knee and sang, "Trot, trot to Boston, trot, trot to Maine . . ." At the end of the song, he dropped her, but he always caught her before she fell.

After he left the boat, Mere kept his clock to remind herself of him. Even now, she remembered how heavy it had felt the first time she held it, and how she could see her face reflected in its surface. The hands were stuck at three o'clock. For Mere, the clock had everything to do with wrong and right. She had to touch the clock when she told a lie. She had to touch it when she had a wrong thought, although the clock was all the way down below deck at the bottom of her locker. It was not easy to touch the clock every time she broke one of her mother's rules. Never lie. Never destroy. Never seek to own. Never wish anyone ill. Faye didn't know that Mere had created her own means of atonement using the clock. But too many trips below might have given Mere away, so over the years the burden of the clock made her vigilant. She was careful in what she said and did, and even more careful about what she thought. Even so, even on the best of days, when she had been careful in thought, word, and deed, she had to touch it at three o'clock. Mere assumed that their life in exile, as Mark called it, must have something to do with her own defects. "Which am I, good or bad?" Mere once asked Faye.

"You're born with one face and give yourself another," Faye replied.

Mere learned this in the same way she learned the names of the twenty-one boys her mother had saved. She knew the names and the harbors where they had been delivered into what her mother called a state of grace. Goderich, Windsor, Hamilton, Kingston. "We could name them all Port Hope!" Faye said.

The stories of the twenty-one boys were altogether mythic for Mere, and the one she loved best was Jimmy's. He had a notebook, and he told Mere he was keeping track of everything she said. He told her he had a grandmother in Virginia who could read a person's fortune in a bottle cap. One night, he talked to Faye when Mere was supposed to be asleep, but she listened from her bunk and learned that Jimmy had gone to Vietnam and then run away. "There's a tunnel under that whole country where they hide out. No lie," he said. "You walk from the top of that country right down to the bottom in that hole, and it's lit up bright as day." Mere's eyes closed and she drifted off, and then woke to another revelation about the tunnel. Jimmy was telling her mother that from what he knew, they ate down there in restaurants and watched movies in enormous caves. They slept down there too, and if they took you in that tunnel, you'd never see the sky again.

She didn't miss the boys, not anymore, although a few of them had come back and visited the boat in one port or another. They arrived, and for a while this boy or that would seem to mean everything. When they appeared, they didn't resemble the people she remembered. Instead, they were grown-up, bearded, long-haired and frightening, liable to hoist her up to a ratline and beg her to scramble to the top "like the monkey you were when you were little." At such times, Mere felt unsure of herself, fearing she might disappoint these heroes by being too awkward, too shy, too big. Faye would change too, becoming less fierce and more obliging. She'd make special things to eat: biscuits, cookies, pies.

Mere's life had been a series of harbors and voyages, never sailing for so long that they ran out of food or diesel, and never stopping anywhere long enough to know the names of more than a few streets: the ones that led to the market, the drugstore, the laundromat, and the library where she was allowed to read the books and magazines, but never to check out anything because that would mean having a library card or putting her name on a form.

For a long time, they were alone. The boys would come and stay, then leave again. They might help for a while, but sooner or later they'd disappear. Then one day when she was below deck playing with her chickens, all of that changed. She had cut some bits of cloth into triangles. They were torn pieces of flags that Faye had liberated from yacht clubs in order to make a quilt. Taking two bright red pieces, she fashioned napkin-size capes for her chickens. There would be a wedding at three o'clock, the time of all her ceremonies; she pictured the clock in the darkness of the locker below, although her father's face was already beginning to fade. Her chickens were going to be married that day, below deck on the *Persephone*, and six-year-old Mere was the captain who would perform the ceremony. They needed their feathers smoothed and their capes straightened, and Mere was seeing to these adjustments when she heard her mother's voice and the thump of feet on the deck overhead. The hatch slid back. Then two bright red sneakers, as bright as the cloths around the chickens' necks—the feet of a bridegroom—stepped down the ladder and into the hold.

He stood there, a boy older than she was but younger than the usual visitors, with scraggly hair and a flushed face. *Someone to play with*, Mere thought, although the boy didn't say anything, just looked with wide eyes at her and at the chickens, which ran to hide under the stove. Mere opened her mouth to speak (it was in her nature to speak, to make conversation with everything: chicken, anchor, or boy), but before she could, Faye leapt with uncharacteristic swiftness down the hatch and into the cabin, lifting the mattress from a bunk. Under the mattress was a wooden plank, and she raised that, revealing a space big enough to hide a grown-up.

"Quick," she said, but the boy was already climbing into the hole. Faye replaced the plank, then the mattress. "Mere," she said, "remember the drill? Get naked," and Mere did as she was told, taking off her own clothes and then beginning to untie the red capes from the chickens, which were still under the stove. "Don't worry about them," Faye said, pounding the mattress that covered the boy's hiding place. Mere lay down on it dutifully and closed her eyes. She had done this before, but never for a boy so young.

They felt the boat rock. A voice yelled, "Hello, down there!" and Faye rushed out of the cabin, taking the narrow hallway into the aft part of the ship and the ladder up into the deckhouse. Lying still as a bone, pretending to sleep, Mere could hear angry voices on deck, but she could not make them out. She saw someone peer through the hatch. She heard Faye talking, talking. Somehow, lying so still, she fell asleep.

She woke to the comforting sound of the engine rumbling beyond the heavy steel bulkhead. The *Persephone* was underway. She opened her eyes. Water splashed against a porthole. Someone had lifted her onto the upper bunk. She thought of the new boy. Had she lost him? She should never have gone to sleep. Mere slipped off the bunk, climbed the ladder to the deck, and saw her mother at the helm. Beside her, seated on one of the benches, the boy was peeling potatoes. He was as thin as the knife he held. The sun had not yet set and the sky around them was red. She hardly noticed it, concentrating her gaze on the boy. "I'm Mere," she said as soon as she was near enough for him to hear.

"Mark," he said, then added, "you're bare naked."

Mere felt her skin turn hot as the sky.

When they were older, Mere would lie with him in the netting below the bowsprit. If they hung their hands out between the holes in the net, Mark's hands would go into the water halfway up his elbows, but Mere's would barely reach the waves. With their hands in the water, they could feel the speed of the boat. Mere would pretend that she was trailing the boat behind her like the long train of a dress. Something solid and grown-up and perfect—a party dress. Later, she felt it was time to leave all that, to take her hands out of the water. She began to dream of a dress made not of water, but of dirt and leaves, a dress busy with the nests of swallows, hives of bumblebees. A dress hemmed with roots.

If the morning was clear, they had breakfast on deck, where Faye would take the helm and tell them a story she remembered, something from a book or a movie she had seen years before. Then Mere and Mark would get to work on the essay of the day, although there would be breaks for boat work. If the wind came up, they might need to douse a sail, and something always needed to be repaired. Meanwhile, the children learned not to ask too many questions. If they did, Faye would divert them to some aspect of the question that she could resolve with the dictionary she kept close at hand, because the answer to life's hardest questions resided there. "That's how I go to the bottom of something," she explained. "I take it apart, examine its stomach and brain. Where does it come from in its beginnings?"

"But why do we live on a boat?" Mere asked.

Faye answered, "Did you know that *to slip the painter* means to leave something behind? Why? What does painter mean?"

"It's the rope attached to the bow that ties the ship to the dock," Mark offered.

"Right," Faye said. "When we slip the painter, we leave the shore behind." And then, as if Mere's question had been one of definition, she continued. "Why does *painter* have so many meanings? There's the one who makes pictures out of paint about whom a writer named Balzac once said, 'I avoid the sight of all paynters lest they shew me the patterne of my pale visage.'" Faye did her best imitation of a Frenchman. "There's the workman who coats boats with color." She rose from the bench beside the helm, pacing, demonstrating with her hands and small stamps of her bare feet.

Mark said, "How do you know all this stuff?" But Mere knew what her mother did at night in her cabin when they were anchored. She read her dictionary and her encyclopedia. Sometimes she used them as storybooks to send Mere to sleep. She kept a little manual of boat types and semaphore signals and buoys, a chart of bird flight patterns and wing spreads. With these, the children could identify anything they saw. With their imaginations, and from a safe distance, they could create boatloads of inhabitants for each of those separate, moving worlds that went sailing or motoring past. They learned to tell the message of a buoy or a lighthouse from its combination of flashing signal and whistle. They learned to imitate these sounds, and once in a while, when Faye was at the helm, one or the other of them would make the noise of a particular buoy from a perch in the cabin below the aft ladder. Then the thrill when Faye—thinking the signal a real warning—called for the boat to come about. "Ready about," she'd yell, and they'd run onto deck to man their stations, Mere on the port side, Mark on starboard—only this time, as their sneakers thumped up the stairs onto deck, they would be laughing.

At eleven, there was an hour of math—this was nobody's strong point, so they made the best of it as a threesome. "If a boat is moving at ten knots, what time will it have to leave Kingston to reach Toronto at noon?"

"Why can't we do airplanes? Or horses!"

"Quiet."

This was not going to be an education that would prepare anyone for the static life of a land-dweller. On the *Persephone*, land-life was scrutinized, especially its history, and when the encyclopedia did not have the answers, Faye invented them. "See, they have Saint Benedict, an Italian monk who died in 547, and Benedict the XI, a pope who died in 1304, and Benedict the antipope and two more popes and another monk and an anthropologist! But where is Benedict Arnold, the most important of the entire bunch and the only one among them who had the courage to change his mind about a king?"

"Wouldn't he be under the A's?" Mark asked.

Faye checked herself, then frowned and continued. "Under the A's, yes. Okay, he was someone who looks into the future in 1770 and sees right off the bat that taxation without representation is the way of all governments! And they won't tell you that. Not in the United States of America. Someone who abandons the revolution right there in its cradle because he figures out that violence isn't worth the cost—they won't tell you about him."

"But you will." Mark was smiling.

Mere turned away. "Wind's coming," she said, moving to her station on the port side. It felt good not to listen to Faye and to move out of reach. It was at this time, when she was ten years old, that Mere began her own log—a description of what she called *Dilemmas*—without once resorting to the dictionary.

Today she tried to teach us a new kind of fractions that I cought onto and Mark didn't. Then we passed a boat and they were pouring stuff in the water that would kill the fish and Faye was quiet angry.

Mark is helping with my script for the play I am writing. We stayed up and talked til really late. Faye was on the helm and couldn't hear us. When she shouted we went up and helped to anchor. It was so dark. I can't lift the chain out but Mark can. We hurred to bed.

Faye made me wear her teeshirt because I was getting burned and I was mad. Then we got to swim. Mark did a cannonball off the deckhouse into the water. Faye didn't swim. She says someone has to be on deck or we could end up with the boat sailing away.

At the age of five, Mere had been able to hoist herself up to the tip of the mast and balance there. She had begun climbing almost as soon as she could walk. Faye had to grit her teeth and remind herself that this was a skill Mere needed as much as land children needed to learn about aiming, scoring and winning. At least there was plenty of teamwork on the *Persephone*, and by the time she was ten, Mere could set and douse the sails, as well as shimmy out on the yardarm to unlash the square sails.

Today was Sunday so we played and did we have fun. Mark was the pirate and I played all the other parts.

Faye talked alot. I HATE Benedict Arnold and his whole revolution.

"You never tell us anything real," Mere said to her mother one afternoon when she was eleven years old. "I'm not talking about history or words or anything, but your real life."

Mark had a sail spread around him like an empty parachute. A threaded needle in his hand, he wore a thick leather glove with a knobby mound on the palm that he pushed against the needle, forcing it into the seam of the sail they'd blown the day before. "Leave it alone," he said.

"She's my mother!" Mere looked at Faye, who was calmly minding the helm. There was little wind now, but the boat rose and fell on swells that were the aftermath of high winds. Faye put up a hand, and Mere thought she would divert their attention, as usual, to something more practical than real life.

"When I was your age," Faye began portentously, "we lived in a town called Erie. I've already told you about that."

"Pennsylvania," Mark added.

"My dad ran a steel company with a lot of men working under him and my mother was rooted to that town. She was a true old-fashioned housewife."

Mere was listening carefully. She was waiting to hear something new. Her grandparents were dead—Faye had already told her that—but what had Faye herself been like? Why had she left her parents when she was so young and run away to live on the *Persephone*?

"When my dad bought the boat," Faye continued slowly, "it was part of his fantasy, part of his attempt at a more elegant life. Mother changed. Just like that. Maybe she was afraid of losing him. Losing us both." Faye stopped short, staring at the two children, then went on haltingly. "She got suspicious and nervous and upset. When the wind blows hard, you need two anchors, one from the bow and one from the stern." She paused and Mere squirmed. Faye was going to lose the thread of the story. It always happened. "How did I get started on this? Anchors—that's what we were talking about." Faye glanced down and blinked. She put a hand up to shade her eyes.

"No, your life," Mere coaxed, afraid that Faye would move on to the anatomy of the anchor: stem, fluke, eyehole.

Faye spoke slowly. "But we were just a family. Living our lives. Mother, father, daughter. Just that." Now she seemed to be talking to herself. "I went to a big school and hated it most of the time, and then we got the boat and my father wanted me to help him sail it." She thought for a minute. "Maybe it was partly for me." She looked straight at Mere. "Because of my loneliness, not having any friends. Anyway, I remember perfectly the first time we went out. Yes. It was like learning to fly and getting to see everything from a distance. All my unhappiness just evaporated. Our town fell away and around me was a space as clean as the sea. I opened my eyes as wide as I could. I held on to the stay and felt the wind on all sides of me, blowing my cotton blouse out like a sail, and then pretty soon, after a few minutes, I couldn't even smell the lake. It was as if I'd known that light, that wind, that smell all my life. Just the way you do now." She focused on Mere without quite seeing her. "And as a matter of fact, it was only seven years later that I was down in the forepeak on a windless day like today giving birth to you."

Faye looked up at the horizon, remembering the two girls at the same time, her twelve-year-old self and herself at nineteen, as if they were both on the ship, one below deck and one above, and it seemed to her that what was different about them was not the fact of age or circumstance, but the quality of wind and light.

Faye shook her head. "Even after I learned to see things from a distance, I still used to cry myself to sleep every night. All because I was lonely. Except for my books, I was really alone. But then I made friends with Jolene."

Mere signaled to Mark. Her gesture said, *Don't ask or she'll stop talking*.

They both knew how to disappear. Mere leaned back against the deckhouse and looked out at the water, which was moving rhythmically under the boat, carrying it up and down rather than forward. Now she learned that Jolene's father worked at the steel mill and that out on the water, away from the other men, Faye's father and Jolene's father became friends. "They both loved this old boat," Faye said, "for their different reasons."

Mark coughed. He couldn't stop himself. But Faye had forgotten the two listeners.

"Well, for my dad the boat was something cherished. He had been a cadet on it, and he'd bought it after the navy stopped using it as a training ship. My mother always said my father was just an old navy man with fancy ideas. Mr. Shore, Jolene's dad, had been in the navy too. For him, the boat was a chance to get away from being a black man in a company town. It was terrible back then."

In spite of her desire to disappear, Mere fidgeted. But for some reason, Faye was not deterred. This was unusual, and Mere allowed herself to stretch her legs, while Faye said that the two men used to take their daughters out on the lake every weekend. The trips had started with the mothers too, but that was a mistake. Mr. Shore had arrived one time with his wife dressed up as if for church, and even Faye's mother had been wearing high-heeled pumps, a flowered dress, and a gold pin in the shape of a rabbit with cut-glass eyes. The two families met in the parking lot, having arrived from their separate ends of town, and there was a moment when the mothers regarded each other, clearly establishing in a shared glance that they were humoring their men. They both knew that a friendship between the two families did not stand a chance. Not in Erie, Pennsylvania. Not then. "I saw my mother flinch when we walked past the entrance to the yacht club," Faye said, "because there was a sign that said Whites Only. We didn't belong to the club. But we had to walk past."

Faye told Mere and Mark how she'd walked ahead of the others, pushing open the chain-link fence and stepping onto the floating wooden dock that rocked under her. "Watch your step," she had said, in the same way her father always did. The men filled the air with talk of the boats around them, the condition of refits, unusual riggings—enough talk to keep them all easy until they reached the *Persephone,* where there was so much to do that no one would feel too awkward.

The two girls ran ahead. Jolene's mother called after her, but then stopped herself, not wanting to scold her daughter for being unladylike and in so doing insult her hosts' daughter. Faye grabbed the line dangling from high up the mast and scrambled, foot over foot, up the side of the ship. Once on board, she opened the locker on deck and pulled out the ladder, lowering it over the side toward the low floating dock. Before she'd leaned it against the hull, Jolene had the dangling rope in hand and was hauling herself aboard. "You've used a line before," Faye said, admiration in her voice. It had taken her several tries the first time.

"What's a line?" Jolene asked.

"It's a rope with a job." Faye repeated her father's words. Jolene was four inches taller than Faye, but thin as a hook. Her skin was a dark brown and her hair pulled back into a tiny ponytail. A few wisps of hair had escaped from the rubber band and stood out from her forehead as if they were electric. It was the same electricity that Jolene had in her smile.

"How old are you?" Jolene asked.

"Fifteen," Faye said. "But my birthday's in October."

"Libra," Jolene said, but Faye had no idea what she meant.

At a loss for words and seeing the adults moving closer to the boat, Faye leapt over the taffrail and up the ratlines toward the top of the mast. Jolene followed, and halfway there she swung her long body past Faye's, beating her to the top. When they were seated side by side, they stared down between their feet, watching one mother and then the next shrug off her husband's offered hand and climb aboard.

"My mother's bad with motion," Faye told Jolene. "She always throws up."

"You ever opened a fortune cookie?" Jolene asked. Faye shook her head. "Mine said I'm twice as lucky." Jolene flashed Faye that smile, and Faye smiled back, showing all her teeth.

"After that," Faye told Mark and Mere, "Jolene and her dad sailed with us every weekend the weather was good." What she failed to add was that the two men did not socialize at other events. Not at the lodge where Faye's father spent his Thursday nights or at the card games where Al Shore met other men on his shift at the steel plant. The two men nodded when they passed each other between the dark machines in the stormy atmosphere of the steel plant. When the union called a strike, they stood on two different sides of the picket lines, but on Sundays they arrived at the harbor separately, from separate neighborhoods, each with a daughter in hand, and walked together down the wooden docks. One of them took the wheel, the other cast off. In a polite way, they came to care for each other, and their daughters were free to invent themselves in each other's presence. Jolene's admiration made Faye feel brave, allowing Faye to do and say the things she usually kept carefully tucked away.

Faye didn't tell the children about the last time they sailed together, although she often thought about it. She and Jolene were down in the main cabin, lying side by side on a bunk, listening to the rush of water streaking on the other side of the hull, as the *Persephone*, under full sail, made her way out of the Erie harbor. Faye ran her finger along the metal, watching how the condensed water would bead and drop like a tear down the inside of the boat. "Are you staying here when you grow up?"

"Uh-huh." Jolene lay beside her, picking at a scab. Flaking pieces fell off, exposing pink flesh. When she shoved her fingernail under the middle of the scab, a clotted plug fell out, and her elbow began to bleed. "Look at that," Jolene said, bending her elbow in and out, like the handle of a pump, slowly forcing more blood out of the wound.

Faye turned from the hull and looked at Jolene's elbow. "Stop moving it."

But Jolene wouldn't or couldn't. She just kept pumping her arm in and out, watching the blood run off her elbow onto the bunk. "Stop it," Faye said. But Jolene's eyes were scared or excited, and the blood was now a dime-size pool.

Faye slid her hand up into the sleeve of her sweater and with the loose end blotted the blood on Jolene's elbow. Jolene stopped pumping. Faye held on. After a few minutes, Faye took the sleeve away, and they both stared at the wound. Jolene twisted her arm around, trying to put her elbow into her mouth. "I gotta lick it to make it clean."

"You can't reach."

Jolene stopped, pointing her elbow at Faye, testing.

Faye leaned closer and took Jolene's elbow into her mouth, pushing her tongue into the small hole. She looked into Jolene's face, and Jolene smiled the electric smile. They stayed like that for a second until they heard Jolene's father shout from up on deck, "Ready about," the call for them to come and help with the sails.

Faye did not tell Mere or Mark about any of this.

Or about what came later, when she and her parents were out for an evening drive. Her mother had the thermos of gin and tonic, which she poured now and then into a glass, along with some ice. Faye's father rattled the cubes in his glass with one hand and drove with the other, and in the glow of oncoming cars, Faye, in the back seat, could see her father begin to sweat. She watched him unbutton the top of his shirt and roll down the window, letting the shriek of summertime into the car, a noise that competed with the static on the radio as Faye's mother fiddled with the knob. Faye lay down across the back seat, watching headlights paint the ceiling of the car. These drives were a weekly event, and it seemed to Faye that they were meant to mollify her mother. But this time, her father drove down the wrong street.

Her father said, "I'm stopping for gas," and then before her mother could react, he added, "where it's less expensive." The car shook and bumped on the rougher streets of south Erie. Faye sat up, staring out the window, hoping to catch a glimpse of this forbidden part of town where her best friend lived. Her father said, "Might stop off for a bit to check on Al. It's been rough on him. And we don't . . ." But Faye wasn't listening. She was smelling the air. Noticing the houses that were no different from hers. Houses just as close together, lawns just as small and tidy, but there were more people on the street and most of them were running.

A column of black smoke poured into the sky, and the sky itself was bright as daylight. There was the scream of a fire truck. Faye's father stopped the car, shoving the door open, and her mother leaned across him, pulling it shut.

"Stay in this car," she said. At the same moment, Faye saw a man in the crowd waving his arms. Her mother's voice kept making words. Her father tried to open the door again, but her mother hissed, "Your daughter is in the back seat."

There was no way to tell Mark and Mere about this. "You're lucky to have only one parent," she said instead. "Having two is confusing."

Faye's father had told her that Jolene died in a fire because Mr. Shore was a union man. Her mother had said, "Your father got that wrong. Al Shore lit the fire himself for the insurance money."

Mere and Mark listened to Faye's breathing. She was lost to them.

Faye thought, *We were there for hours. We didn't do anything. Just sat like that in the car until the traffic cleared.*

✦

When Mere was eleven, Mark started taking her with him when he went ashore to get supplies. Wherever they docked, the two of them left the boat without even throwing down the ladder. The feel of the earth was a joy and a release as they raced up the landing into solid life.

"A mall, let's go find a mall."

"No way! Faye would freak."

"She doesn't have to know." There was something about Mark that Mere didn't understand. A hardness at the edges, and a weakness inside. What was there to be scared about? The worst Faye could do was ground them again, which would mean they couldn't leave their cabins.

And she couldn't ground them both unless she wanted to anchor the boat.

They didn't have enough extra money to do more than buy a bag of licorice for Mere and a pack of cigarettes for Mark to nurse until the next shore leave, lighting one then tapping it out after a puff. Mark said, "We're getting supplies. That's it. No mall."

Walking up the path to the marina, Mere felt sick from the flat calm. In the store, the smell of oily food, floor wax and disinfectant made her queasy, more land-sick. Her cure for this feeling was to stare at the water, but inside the building there wasn't any.

They walked the short aisles, scouring the shelves with hungry eyes. Ropes and hoses next to giant cans of fruit cocktail. Mosquito coils and rubber boots. At the end of one aisle, a girl with bright pink lips and a purse made of fur scowled at Mere. "Mind your own beeswax," said the girl, turning back to a machine standing upright in the corner. The machine made the sounds of small, artificial explosions.

When she left the game, Mark put a quarter in the slot and began to test the buttons. Mere watched, but she wasn't paying attention to what the buttons did or to Mark's score. Instead, she thought, *One day this place will be under water, but Mark and Faye and I will be safe,* because they had heard on the radio about the North Pole melting. She and Mark had decided the *Persephone* would save them. Thinking about the boat and Faye and how safe they were was strangely irritating.

"See my score?" Mark asked, but Mere said, "Watch." She pulled him away from the machines. She walked the aisle of the store slowly, scanning the objects laid out there. She looked at Mark. His eyes said, *Don't,* but he stood where he was frozen and Mere picked something up, stuffing it into the sleeve of her jacket. When she got to the checkout counter, she paused to smile, then moved fluidly out of the store.

"What took you so long?" She was waiting for him outside the marina.

"Why'd you do that? You could get us busted."

"Music belongs to the air."

"That's bullshit," Mark said.

The cassette in her sleeve held music that Mere, without a tape deck, would never hear. Still, it was music and it was hers. She buried it under her boots in the bottom of her locker, and touched the clock to make amends for ownership.

When the cassette disappeared a few days later, she didn't say a word to Mark. Between them, certain things were never mentioned. He didn't have a mother of his own, and she wondered how he could grow up without someone to belong to. How could he know himself? He could quote dates and places, and he had names on the tip of his tongue. He helped her with the essays Faye assigned. And with the rules. If he had taken her cassette, he was making a point. If music belonged to air, she couldn't complain about losing it. That day, Mere threw his sacred collection of Spiderman comics overboard.

The next time she touched the clock, it was to make amends for taking revenge.

A few days later, the *Persephone* docked in Belleville. An

old man sat on the dock listening to a small tape deck, his fishing line drooping in the water near the stern of the boat. When Faye ducked her head below deck and said she was going for a nap and that Mark and Mere should get the supplies, Mark went below too, while Mere waited for him restlessly on the dock. When he reappeared, he swung himself up onto the ratlines and then jumped to shore. "Mind if we listen to this?" he asked the fisherman, pulling the stolen cassette from his pocket.

The man nodded, lifting his pole, alert to the fish now that he had an audience. Mark slipped the tape into the box. *Where will we run, when the rains come?* The music wailed out of the box.

Mere's face, half smile, half laugh, was a moon of light. Mark took one of her hands in his and put an arm around her waist. He sent her spinning out at the end of his arm, then twirled her back again. "You're light on your feet," he said, using words he remembered his father using. When the song was over, he stepped back.

Mere stooped to the tape player and popped the cassette out, stashing it in her pocket, then they walked together into town.

THE PAMPHLET

In a life of sleepless nights, the one Faye spent waiting for Mere was the longest. She ranged the boat, bow to stern, fumbling with lines, glaring at unpolished cleats, fuming over stains on the deck. She became concerned with the damaged and imperfect minutiae of her surroundings, as if by staunching all wounds—visible and invisible—she could will Mere to her side. Mere, without whom she could not live. Mere, who was all that Faye had ever wished for: skin, hair, animated voice, bony ankles and wrists, raised eyebrow. Mere, who was lost now in some incomprehensibly dangerous way. Faye began breaking down the parts and complexion of Mere, as if her daughter were dead—although that thought was unthinkable and had to be kept at bay. Part of this delirium was grief, another part was fury. What had this marvelous, stupid girl done? How thoughtless, selfish, unkind had she become? She had run off with her father—Faye was certain of that now.

Waiting, trapped on the boat, Faye knew that she could

be discovered at any moment. She might hear the crack of willow branches as men approached (there would be many of them), coming at last to lock her away from her child for good. Forever. Mere was endangering both of them with her foolish game. Or had Merril told his daughter about Faye? Exposed her as Faye had never exposed herself? If so, what must Mere think of her? Consequences. Everywhere, the snare of consequences. *Oh God, what must I give up this time? What more am I required to pay?* And Faye thought of her own mother with guilt and pain, remembering the day she'd walked out of her mother's house and never looked back. Of course, Faye had intended to go back, she'd meant to, and she'd called . . . *I know you've been worried to death* . . .

Faye remembered a time when she'd left Mere on a piece of empty shoreline—where was it? Mere had demanded shore leave, had stormed around, beating her small fists against the deckhouse, finally bursting into tears. Faye had doused the sails and steered into the shallows, telling Mere to go ahead and swim to shore if she craved so much to put her feet on land. Then Faye had sailed off, leaving Mere alone. Someone was on deck with Faye, one of the boys. Jimmy, yes, because she remembered his telling her that it was cruel, what she was doing. "Her only company's the gulls," Jimmy had said, shaking his head, although he was familiar enough with Faye's method of mothering. An hour or so later, when they sailed back, Mere was sitting with her knees pulled to her chest. "I wanted to buy you a stupid birthday present!" she hissed, refusing to budge, threatening to stay there forever, until Jimmy dove at her and hoisted her up on his back. Mere was shouting, "I'll never do anything for your stupid birthday ever again!"

And she hadn't.

In the galley, Faye poured herself a glass of bourbon and sat at the pullout table, which had known so many hands, so many elbows, so many knives. When had the bourbon come aboard? The bottle nearly empty now. It must have sat gathering dust in the cabinet behind the sink for four or five years, whenever she'd last had adult company.

She found herself sobbing, surprised by the noise of it, and hit the table with her fist, as if it might crack open to reveal her child's face, as if Mere had been hiding all these hours. And then the thought came to her distinctly, and she ran to check under each and every bunk, tossing the mattresses off, then ran up onto deck, throwing open the bucket locker and frightening the chickens, who had not flown away to liberty as she had expected but were roosting sleepily around the warm base of the stovepipe.

The bourbon was having its effect, and she stumbled against things and cursed, heard footsteps and knew the men had come. Near the bow, a shadow loomed, and she checked its density, its outline, recognizing Mark. So they had not come for her yet. Maybe they would not. Unless she still had to appease the gods. Or God. But she could not believe in God because if she did, it meant only that she was damned, and this terrible loss was the proof.

When the sun began its dreary rising over the eastern end of the harbor, she felt more frightened than ever, since Mere had been truly away from her for a full night. And now she must think, although her eyes were starched with dry ache, her throat hurt, and her brain felt immobilized. Where could she turn? Only to Merril, who had stolen her daughter. Only to Merril, whose house was surrounded by the FBI. Only to Merril, who, if he didn't have Mere, would at least know what to do.

✦

The Cherry Street Grill sat beside the wall of freighters at the eastern end of Toronto harbor, a nondescript room in a sagging building. It was a place with a pay phone outside by the door and a waitress who didn't ask questions. It had once been a place for Faye's draft dodgers to meet contacts. Now, on an October morning in 1982, with Mere missing somewhere in the city, it was the first place Faye thought to send Mark looking for Merril Holmes. The fact that the last of the draft dodgers had vanished into Toronto years before, and the possibility that the diner they had once frequented might no longer be operating, did not occur to Faye when she ordered Mark to get himself over there. It was an order that measured the extent to which she'd lost her connection to the world.

Another measure was her instruction to Mark. "Ask about Merril Holmes. Find out where he lives. Then go get Mere. Bring her back fast. But make sure no one follows you on the way back to the boat." She gave Mark four dollars and fifty cents, packed him a lunch of hard-boiled eggs and carrot sticks, and offered no further explanation. She was doing anything she could to keep moving, stop thinking. What if Mere had gone somewhere else? Wouldn't that be worse than going with Merril? What if she was wandering Toronto's streets? Mere, who had never left her for so long as an hour—or that's how it felt to Faye. And Merril. Why come down and ask her to take him underground, and when she said no, steal her child? It didn't make sense. "This is urgent, life or death," she told Mark as he jumped off the boat and headed down the path toward the ferry, which would take him across the harbor to the Cherry Street Grill.

✦

Mere lay in a large bed, listening to the sounds of morning, the cry of a bird outside and the popping metal explosions like a dozen hammers banging inside the radiator, much larger than the radiators they had on the boat. Everything was larger: the window huge and rectangular, with a long piece of canvas that rolled down from the top to cover it. Mere sat in bed and searched for a way to roll the canvas up, but when she touched its cord, it startled her by snapping up like a tongue. There was a square red carpet on the deck—no, the floor. The bed, so much roomier than her own narrow bunk. And there were paintings on the walls. At the foot of the bed hung a picture of a man, his head tilted to one side, leaning over a guitar.

Mere did not remember dreaming, only that the night before she'd wandered through the rooms of a house that was large enough to hold seven or eight *Persephone*s. The bedroom was hot, and she thought of opening the window through which sunlight poured like egg yolk. Sunny-side up, the way her mother ate her eggs, so she could sop the yolks up with her toast. There was a tree outside, and Mere wondered whether anyone would notice if she climbed it later, before she went back to the boat. Where was Merril? Her father!

All these years she'd been trying to decipher his story. He had come across the lake with her mother, so he must have been like the other boys she carried who were trying to escape the war. But this account had never made sense to her. If he had a daughter, he wouldn't be drafted—she knew that much. So why had her father vanished into Canada? And now, to find him living inside the vaulted rooms of this house. Were the other boys—all twenty-one of them—so lucky? She'd always imagined them wandering the shores, with nothing but a knapsack and their wits to keep them going.

She heard a door slam and then a female voice called up. "Merril?"

Mere listened closely. At last she heard her father answer. "Up here. In the study."

A few times in the course of her brief life, Mere had slept on the land, but the absence of rocking and groaning had kept her awake. Also the change in smell, although none of these things had occurred to her as particular. Mere was observant in her own way, but she was not a child to analyze her surroundings. She had not had enough to compare those surroundings to. She had never spent time with adults other than Faye, did not know their rhythms of speech or the signals that indicated trouble. She heard a door open somewhere nearby and then the voice. "What in hell was the meaning of the note you left downstairs?"

"Jesus, I thought I threw it away . . ." When she heard a door shut, and couldn't hear the rest of Merril's answer, she got out of bed and crept down the hall to the closed door.

". . . but I didn't expect you back. Not now. How was Montreal, your flight?"

"I don't want to talk about my flight. I want to talk about yours." The voice was angry. And the words sounded strange, not quite English.

Mere was wearing her underpants and a shirt Merril had given her the night before. She suddenly felt exposed and anxious, the morning with her father ruined by an angry visitor while she had been waiting for him to come into her room, wake her up, talk about what they would have for breakfast. She had already pictured the scene, although her idea of a kitchen was her mother in the galley beside the stove, stirring and talking about which sails needed to be sewn or what ideas she had for the essay of the afternoon. Sometimes when she thought no one was listening, Faye made conversation with the cooking spoon. Her old confessor, she called it.

Stir with a knife, trouble and strife. It was something Faye said, and it came into Mere's head as she listened to her father's voice. "I had to disappear. We've talked about this. You knew it could happen."

"Was I supposed to expect to ever see you again? I forget."

Mere stepped back, her stomach knotted.

"I said in the note I'd find a way to get in touch. You know I would do that."

"You had a plan. All along, you had a plan and you

never told me." A pause. "*Je ne veux pas disputer!*" Then a choked sound.

"I don't want to fight either. Going to the boat was a bad idea. I've got a new plan, El."

Through the banister, Mere could see Rogue scratching at the front door. She heard, "Does this also involve leaving me?" Where was the bathroom? Mere couldn't remember. She did not want to knock on the closed door while a strange lady was in there talking to Merril. Maybe it would be best, after all, to go back to the room and lie down on the bed.

Who was this lady?

In the bedroom, she stood at the dresser, studying her face in a small mirror. Was she pretty? No one had ever told her. She picked up a smooth red box and opened it. There was nothing inside. *What's it for?* Mere wondered, going back to the bed and lying down.

A few minutes later, the door swung open and Merril put his head in. "How'd you sleep?"

"It's so quiet." Then she glanced up at the man with the guitar. "I like him. Who was the painter? Was it Balzac?"

"You'll have to ask Ellie. It's her favourite. Actually I want you to meet Ellie, she's sort of your stepmother." He pulled in his breath, pursing his lips as if sealing a deal with himself.

"Stepmother."

"Anyway" —he pulled back the blanket— "she's downstairs right now making some breakfast."

"Are you coming down too?" Mere stood up. The T-shirt he'd given her came all the way to her knees.

"I'll be around. I've got something I have to do." He pointed to the clothes she'd left on the floor. "Put those on before you go down."

Seated at a table with the dog under her bare feet, Mere compared her new surroundings to what she had always known. The table was covered with a soft blue cloth. The window was covered with curtains. The curtains were tied back from the glass with red tassels, and the woman at the stove was not like her mother, not at all. She wore a bright orange jacket and a short skirt, and she wore black stockings so thin and delicate that Mere could see her pale skin underneath. She was short, but ample. A generous curly wave of black hair, a round face with big dark eyes, a big bosom, and wide hips. She wasn't fat, Mere decided, but she gave off a feeling of bounty, plenty to go around.

Mere sniffed the air and wondered why her father's house was so large. Did he often take people in? Accustomed to reading the weather by pressing her ear to surfaces, she put her head on the table and listened, but except for the tiny hum of something mechanical, the house was unnervingly silent. Only Rogue stirred, then pawed once at her leg. "He might be pretty hungry by now," Mere said, but the lady with the curly black hair didn't seem to hear.

On the tiled counter, a TV was silently playing. Long sweeps of blue arrows and red swirls crossed a map of Canada and the lakes. It was exciting to think of herself on land instead of water. Mere remembered her mother's description of leaving land for the first time, when her father had bought the *Persephone*. Flying, she had called it. Now Mere was as far from the boat as she had ever been. Suppose she decided in an instant to go back. How would she know the way? She put both feet against Rogue's warm stomach because for a moment she felt afraid.

The person on TV moved her mouth, pointing out clouds and lightning bolts. Why didn't she talk? Why didn't she point to the weather over the lakes? Mere had spent hours listening to radio transmissions of Great Lakes' weather. Their lilt and repetition comforted her. She'd been allowed, from an early age, to record the daily weather conditions in the log. When she thought of Faye's phrase "right livelihood," she always imagined herself as a farmer or a weather reporter.

Thinking of Faye, Mere felt a twinge of guilt. Where was her mother now? At Lighthouse Cove? And what about Mark? The thought of him made Mere feel worse. But Mark would have to help Faye understand that being with her father for these hours was something Mere had to do.

The lady with the curly black hair, whose name was Ellie, moved to the stove. Mere watched her pour batter into a skillet. "Pancakes?" Mere asked nicely. She had not been able to think of what to say to Ellie since her father had left the kitchen. "This is Mere," he had said, not mentioning that Mere was his daughter. "This is Ellie. I'll leave you to get acquainted."

"Crepes," said Ellie, and began singing under her breath. It was a song about walking on the moon. Mere slipped out of her chair and got down on the floor with the dog. From under the table she said loudly, "That's the year before I was born," to make conversation. She had been taught to be polite.

"What's that?"

"Walking on the moon. It was one year before I was born in the middle of Lake Erie."

There was no response.

"How long are you staying here?" Mere asked, putting her head out, then pulling herself to her feet. It was the sort of question she might have asked one of the boys who appeared on the boat now and then.

"This is where I live. I own this house."

Mere was confused. "Did you know he had me?" she could have asked, but the woman spoke again.

"Does your mother know you're with us?" When Mere didn't answer, Ellie said, "Do you want to call her, tell her you're here?"

"Call her. How?"

"On the telephone."

"Oh," Mere said, surprised now by Ellie's confusion. "We don't have one of those. We live on a boat."

"Right," Ellie said, then she lifted the thin pancake off the skillet and slid it onto a plate painted with flowers.

Why put flowers on a plate when the food was just going to cover them up?

"You need a haircut." Ellie poured more batter. "Your hair's in your eyes. Don't you want people to see your face?"

"You make your words sound different," Mere said quietly.

"My little bit of accent, you mean?"

"What's accent?"

"People talk according to their backgrounds. I grew up in Quebec." Ellie paused. "My mother spoke French, my father spoke English."

"How did they talk to each other?"

"Good question." Ellie laughed, but then she didn't answer it.

Mere wondered if she had a lake accent. "I AVOYD AL PAINTEERS LEAST they SHOE me my PAIL VISHOON."

Ellie looked confused.

"Balzac," Mere said. "Did he paint the man with the guitar?"

"Ah, no." Ellie smiled now. "Picasso. Anyway, Balzac was a writer."

"Oh." Mere took this in. "I believe it's about time for Rogue's breakfast," she said, already planning what she would say next. She wanted to find out if she should have a wash, which was something she hadn't done, and why the TV was without sound, and whether there were other programs to watch, and whether she was allowed to put maple syrup on her crepes. When her father came back, she would ask him to cut her hair before she went back to the boat. And while she was at it, she was going to ask him who Liza was.

"I'm going to my cabin for a second," Mere said, then suddenly felt ashamed of presuming that the place where she'd slept was hers. "I mean . . ." What if Ellie told her father? What if the two of them laughed at Mere for thinking she belonged to this magical house?

"Put the dog out. He's getting fur all over the place."

"But he hasn't eaten yet."

"His food's on the porch."

Mere left Rogue on the porch, carefully tied down. Back inside, she went up the wide staircase and down the hall, past a closed door that made her think her father might be on the other side. He'd been fun the night before, picking up the telephone and ordering a special dinner. "Chinese, how does that sound?"

She'd been surprised when a man arrived at the door with their dinner in little white boxes. Each box had a thin metal handle, like a bucket. Had the food come all the way from China? She'd wished that Mark could be there. They ate their dinner with chopsticks, Merril making a great show of teaching her how to eat. "Don't stab at the food," he said. "Lift it up from underneath, if you have to." When she did it right, he thumped her on the back. "You're a quick study." He'd taken some of the food, rinsed the meat off under the tap, and fed it to Rogue. After dinner, they had each chosen a little folded cookie with a slip of paper inside. He said it was her fortune. Now she couldn't remember exactly what her fortune had said, but that was okay—she'd set it on the table beside her bed. When she went back to the boat, she'd tape it into her book of *Dilemmas*.

She pushed open the door into the study, but no one was there. She moved over to the desk. It was his. There were papers in piles. She lifted a photograph of a group of men in shorts and T-shirts, all in matching colors. Rosedale League '81, it said on the back. Opening drawers was strictly against the rules, she knew that. But the rules in here might not be the same as her mother's. Besides, she deserved to snoop a little bit because she was trying to understand who her father was, since her mother hadn't told her anything about him for all these years. She slid open the drawer. On top of a pile of letters and papers lay a black gun. She knew she shouldn't touch it. Faye had explained to her about guns. Mere slid the drawer shut. On the desk was a metal box with white dogs painted on it, and inside were candies wrapped in pink-and-black waxed paper. She untwisted the paper and put a candy in her mouth. Licorice. She would hold the taste as long as she could without chewing. A machine on the floor exhaled vapor. It seemed to her that the house ran itself, required no vigilance—unless her father was busy somewhere, out of sight, tending to it. A paper had dropped to the floor, and she picked it up, uncurling it like a leaf.

> *They want to know the following: for what are the macaws needed? I have told them breeding. You should stick to that. By the way, Howard released minus 5 million pesos. Regards.*

Dropping the paper back on the floor, Mere slipped out the door and moved down the hall to find out what her fortune said.

✦

At the Cherry Street Grill, no one knew Merril Holmes. This was not a surprise to Mark, who had stepped off the boat often enough to know something about the size of the world. But finding this man was important to Faye, who'd been rattling around all night. If tracking him down brought Mere back, it might even ease the tight feeling in Mark's stomach. He stepped out of the restaurant, lit a cigarette, and stood cleaning the grease from under his fingernails, waiting for a plan to come to him. Then he saw a telephone in a glass booth and the phone book dangling on a coiled metal line. There was his answer. It was easy. In the booth someone had scrawled in thick red pen, THE WORLD HAS ENDED, and someone else had written, FAT CHANCE! The messages made Mark laugh, and his breath sent mist around his head.

In the phone book, he found Merril's name and address on Cluny Drive.

He knew Yonge Street. It was the one that went straight up from the harbor, longest street in the world, a line from the lake all the way to Hudson's Bay. He'd walk up it and ask directions. He carried eight cigarettes, the four dollars and fifty cents from Faye, and four books of matches he'd liberated from the counter at the Cherry Street Grill. *Fire belongs to the air*. It was ten in the morning. He'd already eaten the boiled eggs. Opening the first book of matches, Mark tore one off and lit it. He waited until he'd crossed the street before lighting the next one. Then, for each block, he lit another small flame, cupping his palm around the matchbook in case of a breeze. In this way, he kept track of distance, walking under the raised highway and into the steel heart of the city.

Cars rushed overhead, and Mark thought he would like to be in one of them or sailing away watching the city's towers sink into the unforgiving lake. This thought of the lost city and its inhabitants drowning pleased him, until he remembered that Mere was somewhere in that city. When he reached Yonge, he headed north, once more lighting a match and throwing it over his shoulder into the street. The drowning would come soon enough.

It had begun to snow. Tiny flakes scattered themselves around, and Mark shivered in his denim jacket. Walking faster to keep warm, shoving his hands in his pockets, he stopped a man to ask directions. At Queen Street, he watched people in suits and coats and bright athletic clothes move ceaselessly from the street into an immense building with a glass entrance. As if there were answers inside to every question, they pushed themselves into the building's shelter, removing scarves and gloves, unbuttoning jackets and coats. He followed them and found himself in a cathedral of shops.

People were moving along, up and down escalators, between lights and windows and mirrors that magnified the movement of fur and fabric. An electrical charge. A boy brushed past him with his cap pulled down over his forehead. *Furtive*, Mark thought. *He's picked up something that doesn't belong to him.* Mark's heart pounded fitfully and he jumped aside. Outside, he had felt the hard eyes of other pedestrians, but in here no one looked at him. In the heat and anonymity, a flock of Canada geese flew overhead, and it was a moment before he realized they were hanging on strings. *Someone has gone to the trouble of making these geese, when there are real ones circling the city looking for a patch of ground to land on, something to eat.*

Then he was not thinking of Mere or geese, but remembering the time his father had taken him to another mall. It was in Hamilton. Christmastime. "Matthew had just turned five," he said out loud. Saying his brother's name made his throat ache, as if the sound didn't fit there and had forced its way out. Matthew. For Mark, the unacknowledged treat of the event was not shopping or visiting the mall, but simply being with his father. "Not that he doesn't love you," Mark's mother always said, "but he has to make the world better," which meant being a policeman. But that morning, he was taking the boys into town without their mother, so they could buy her a Christmas present. In the stores, the racks and shelves seemed too close together, but Mark tried to feel happy about the chocolate bar he'd been given as a treat. Matthew sat in a plastic racing car and his father put a dime in a slot to make the car shake. Mark ate the chocolate bar. In one hand, he clutched a paper bag with the silver pendant he had picked out for his mother. In the other hand, he held the melting chocolate. He could taste this moment, and he could remember his brother spinning the little pretend wheel, his father bending down, licking his handkerchief and wiping the stray chocolate from around Mark's mouth. Mark had thought then that his mother would like her pendant.

Now, in the middle of the glass cathedral, Mark touched his mouth, feeling the place where the chocolate had once been, the sweetest bit because it was the last trace. He pushed himself through the crowd back onto the street.

✦

"Did you get something in your tummy?" Merril touched Mere's hair and the touch made her as uncomfortable as the word. *Tummy*. He had finished his workout in the basement, he told her—simple weights and a chinning bar in front of a small TV. "Keeps my blood pressure down" was what he said, adding that making ends meet might be important, but he wasn't about to die in the process.

After the weights and chin-ups, he drank orange juice, then coffee. "Taken here, in my best room." He gestured at the kitchen. "Where's Rogue?"

Mere pointed to the porch. "She told me to put him out there."

"Well, Ellie's not crazy about strays, but don't worry." Merril was moving around in the kitchen as if he needed a way out. He kept looking at the door, then glancing at the windows. "Come over here. I want to show you something."

This was the third time he'd called her over to a window. First, it was the neighborhood itself that he wanted to show her, pulling her over to the big window in the front of the house. Next, it was the side door and the ravine, the path he'd taken down to the boat.

"What are you up to?" Ellie asked crossly, entering the kitchen. "Showing her off? Is that your plan?"

"Shut up," Merril told her. "I'm showing off my pear tree." He raised his eyebrow to Mere as Ellie abruptly left the room again. "Or did I show it to you last night?" In fact, he couldn't bring the previous evening into focus. There were mornings when time did this, mornings when he wasn't accountable. What exactly had happened the day before? Whatever it was, Faye would never come after the girl. On the other hand, she wouldn't go off and leave Mere entirely. Faye would still be waiting down at the harbor. This thought stirred something in him. He looked at Mere standing beside him at the window. She was by right half his. "It was planted before the house was here," he said. "It's part of an old orchard. The last tree."

Mere nodded, although it was clear to Merrill that she had never been near an orchard, never picked an apple or a pear. Never eaten at a table in the kitchen of a house. Her body just barely restrained a wild energy that reminded him of a time when he had been equal to anything. "You're more like me than your mother, you know that?" he said, and in truth he felt as sorry for Mere as for himself.

Mere said that she and her mother were completely, completely different. "I never want to be like her," she said. But the moment the words were out of her mouth, she looked around the kitchen. No clock to touch. She excused herself and got up and went to the bathroom with its loud fan that rattled to life as soon as she turned on the light. She could not put soap in her mouth because she had just eaten and throwing up would be wasteful. Instead, she opened a bottle that said Listerine and took a good, strong mouthful of regret, closing her eyes and swallowing. She wanted to be with Faye, not against her, but it was hard to be with her mother in her father's house.

When she came out of the bathroom, Merril was talking into the telephone. She saw tension in his straight back before she heard it in his voice. "She's here right now."

Mere stepped back into the dark, quiet bathroom.

"Yeah, hey, of course I did. I wouldn't do it without her

consent, would I?" There was a long pause, and then a note of pleading came into Merril's voice. "I'll just stop by, that's all. Five, ten minutes."

"What grade are you in?" Merril asked when Mere stepped out of the bathroom. "Or do you even go to school?"

Mere said, "Rogue doesn't like the cold. Maybe we should let him inside." She stepped toward the patio. She could see the back fence of the house and beyond that the towers of the city.

"Don't go outside. I don't want you wandering around out there by yourself."

So there were rules in her father's house too. She did as he said, moving across the kitchen. "Who's Liza?" she asked then.

Merril decided to tell her, wanted to explain some of it. *Why not?* he thought. *Kids are tougher than most people think. Resilient.* Hadn't he survived his mother's squalid little life, the armies of men who'd sent him out to play, locked the door? Made it through on his own wits. Lived in a real home now, with a yard. Shit, he nearly had an actual wife. And finally this kid, who was different from what he'd thought, but tough, like she ought to be.

"Who's Liza?" she asked again, her feet firmly planted, her arms crossed over her chest.

He wanted to tell her, but he couldn't. Maybe the whole house was bugged, and there was no place he could say it without their hearing. If they overheard, there'd be nothing left for him to use in his own defense.

Suddenly he wanted to do something to make her

understand what her old man was made of. "I want to show you something," he said, steering her toward the basement.

✦

Noon, and they hadn't come back. She should leave the boat, pack the important things: the money, the ship's log, any evidence . . . All this was running through her head as she found the old duffel bag in the wrong place, slightly mildewed but serviceable—when had she last packed anything?—and began stuffing clothes into it from the drawers in her cabin. *Other women do this when they're having a baby*, she thought. In the deckhouse, Faye rummaged through the drawer of the chart table, the same chart table her father had used. Here, the good fortune of a cigarette butt! How old? She stuffed it in her pocket and took the log, squashing it into the duffel bag sideways. She would stuff the cash between its pages. Best to carry no identification, but there were the old licenses, American, for the *Persephone*. And her father's pilot's license. And . . . the pamphlet. Still intact! "How to Make a Revolution," it said in thick block letters. She shoved it into her pocket. *Incriminating*, she thought. *Evidence*. She would not smoke the cigarette butt until she was in a safe place. She would not attend to Mark's or Mere's things. Not yet. They could do that when they came back. First, she had to stash the duffel.

She moved to the bow and shimmied down a rope into the shallow water. Instinctively she coiled the rope and tossed it back on the deck. If the men came, it wouldn't be easy for them to get on board.

Soon she was above the boat, looking down at it, watching it from the relative safety of the lighthouse platform. From up here, she would see them if they came. *The men.* That was how she thought of them. When Mark came back with Mere, she would see them too. The bag was safe. She had left it under the lighthouse stairs.

She tried to think, smoking the butt and occasionally turning her exhausted gaze from the boat and the path to look past the pine trees, out over the lake and the three tall radio towers anchored to pilings in the water. She imagined the signals they were sending into the city. She was so tired, with a headache blooming behind her eyes, but if she concentrated hard enough, her thoughts might travel that distance too. *Mere,* she thought, *come back,* remembering the first time her daughter had climbed the rigging on her own. "You wait here," Mere had said, and Faye had dutifully stood, heart in her throat, watching her daughter disappear into the rigging. Her head tilted back, squinting against the sun and the deep blue of the sky, she'd seen Mere's body crawling across the web of ropes like a small, dark spider moving toward its prey, so hungry was her daughter to reach the top of the mast. When she did, when her feet were firmly on the spreaders, Mere called down, "I did it," her voice echoing against the red cliffs of the Niagara River. "Clip on your harness," Faye called.

Now, looking at the three orange towers, her head throbbing, Faye began to hear other echoing voices: that moment years before when she and her mother had knelt in the wet earth of the garden troweling out patches of soil the size of iris bulbs. "Sprinkle in the bone meal," her mother had said, and Faye had wondered, without asking, why irises needed bones. Her father's hands on a deck of playing cards, his face moving into hers, and the sharp, spicy ether of his breath. "Is that the card you picked?" Mere on the mast, "I did it." Faye took the pamphlet out of her pocket, "How to Make a Revolution," recalling the bullhorn, the boy in dark glasses. *Do you want to stop the war?*

In the spring of the year, her life started. During a math exam. They had barricaded the door to her classroom and she'd sat riveted in her chair, eyes drawn to the boy's face, to his dark glasses, to the bullhorn, although students were hiding under desks, and a few had wrestled with three people dressed as skeletons who blocked the door. A skeleton held the teacher in an arm lock. Others danced on the desks. *Why take a test when you will soon be dead?* What was the point of math when they were killing innocent students from America along with villagers in Vietnam?

It had occurred to her, as she sat in rapt silence watching the boy, that she'd never seen such anger displayed anywhere, although there must be plenty of it around—enough to fuel this crazy, exciting afternoon along with a terrible, unfair war. She realized that she had not felt such a rush of horror and excitement since the time she'd watched Jolene's house burn down. On that day, the thrill had upset her. She was ashamed of it and denied its gravity. She had not known, at first, that it was her best friend's house, only that from then on something powerful and unrelenting was going to keep happening to her. Nothing would ever again be the same. She'd been locked inside her father's car, unable to move, with all those people running toward the flames, and she had felt the thrill and then the shame.

In the classroom, the demonstration was over in a few minutes. The boy with the glasses and the bullhorn simply handed her a pamphlet. The shouting stopped and the three skeletons at the door threw it open, as the other protesters, all of them, ran out, hurling themselves down the hall. It was over, though she would not forget it. That afternoon, she walked down the dock, passing the Erie yacht club, the hulls of the racing yachts lifting on the small waves, their thin rigging pinging and ticking against metal masts. With a delicacy the *Persephone* would never possess. And there the boat sat. Too bulky and tall for the wooden docks, it was held by metal chains to a concrete pier where its steel hull chafed and groaned. The wind seemed to be urging the old boat to quit its mooring. Her father had been dead a year and she hadn't sailed the boat even once. Still holding the pamphlet, she found the key inside the stovepipe and worked it into the lock. The hatch screeched after a winter and a summer of disuse, exhaling the bitter musk of diesel, mold, and damp wood as she climbed down the ladder and into the main cabin. Taking a match from the drawer and twisting the knob on the oil lamp to expose the wick, she brought an eerie light into the airless galley.

The pamphlet was shocking. It announced boldly that she was on the road to a lifetime of low-end jobs that would further the war in Vietnam and the oppression of people in other parts of the world. The light from the oil lamp poured over the badly printed, smudged paper, but by the time she put the pamphlet down, Liza Greene, eighteen years old and not quite finished with high school, was beginning to reinvent herself. A new life, like a bulb pouring its energy into shoot and blossom, was beginning to emerge, drawing nourishment from soil, bone, and root. Instead of patriots, the boys in her class who were about to be sent to Vietnam were victims. Yet perpetrators too. *All of us*, she thought, *have been duped*. But thanks to the fervor of a few outsiders, total strangers (a boy in dark glasses, the angry skeletons), she had been given a look at the truth.

She started by asking her classmates if they knew who the skeleton-people were, and some of them seemed to know more than she did, to have firmer opinions, but none of them led her to the pamphlet's source.

One day, as she pushed open the solid oak doors of the high school, dragging her heavy bag of books and gym clothes, she saw him again. He stood at the bottom of the steps, long legs, long arms—even his hands that held a stack of pamphlets were long. He was too tall for his body. Long face and long hair. "I saw you last week," she said.

"Shh." He put a hand over her mouth.

She had the sudden desire to put her tongue between his fingers. Up close, his gaze was direct rather than angry.

"I'm Gil," he said. "Are you ready?"

That night, she followed his directions to a colonial house set back from the street by a wide lawn and a flagstone pathway. A layer of ice and snow covered the lawn, and as she walked up the path, she noticed a shovel frozen in a bank of ice as if months ago someone had thrown it down in disgust. Such a wealthy house, and yet this shovel signaled that things were not, as her mother would say, being looked after. There was no light on above the porch, but she made out the doorbell. A girl her own age answered, her hair covered in a flowered scarf tied in back. "We don't ring bells around here," she said, then, "I'm Rachel."

As they padded down the carpeted hallway, she noticed photographs: a gray-haired couple with their arms around the girl. Parents. There would be no more photographs of her own father, she thought, and suddenly his death felt real to her. *Never*. A new word. And his ashes were still on the boat, in the chart table, although he had wanted to be scattered on the lake.

Liza followed Rachel to the kitchen, where she found Gil in the center of a group. He had a bag of dope in his hands and was running his fingers through it. He smiled when he saw her—"Glad you made it"—and introduced her to the others. A squat boy with acne. The one called Pegasus, who sat with a guitar between his legs. Another pair of legs stuck out from under the sink. "Ahab," Gil said. "He's fixing the sink. We screwed it up, and Rachel's folks are out of town."

"Ahab?"

"He's chasing down white mother country imperialists," Rachel explained, laughing. She spoke with a confidence Liza envied.

Liza tried to connect the faces of the people in front of

her with the skeletons, but now they looked like everyone else, only looser, less tended. The men had long hair and beards, more or less. The women wore jeans, work shirts, and boots. She regretted her gray wool dress. When the joint was passed around, she watched, then sucked back a long sweet breath and almost instantly felt her shoulders relax. She slid quietly down the front of the stove. "Watch your hair," someone said, because she had turned the burner dial on her way down.

Gil was exhorting the others to come up with a name for the newsletter they were planning to publish.

"Hammer," offered a bulldoggish woman with eyes that were two different sizes. She was sitting in a corner.

"As in sickle?" the pimpled boy said sarcastically.

"I like it!" Rachel said.

Pegasus fingered a couple of chords and raised a surprisingly sweet high voice, singing a few notes. But no one was listening.

The body under the sink slid out and sat up across the floor from Liza. His gray eyes met hers. "We could cut all this crap about print and start broadcasting," he growled. He was barrel-chested, strong, and dark-haired. His broad face had a wide nose and a generous mouth. "I can make an antenna out of tubing, pick up a mike, set up a transmitter out of low power parts."

Gil said, "You're dreaming again, my man."

"It takes dreams to build a dream." Gray eyes flashed.

"You want to build or bring down?"

Liza could feel that they were the two centers around which the group turned.

Rachel said, “Broadcasting is a more intense communication.”

Gil snorted at her. “If you want intense, blowing things up is better than print.”

Pegasus was snapping his fingers. “Give me more rock and roll!” He seemed to be the clown, offering up comedy whenever there was tension.

Liza could not believe her good fortune in being here. She was standing in a room where people were talking about politics. About action. They didn’t seem to mind her listening.

“Under the regs, it’s pure and legal to broadcast on the AM band without getting a license,” Ahab pointed out.

Gil was getting impatient. “As long as you take up only a milliwatt of band space that nobody more than a block away can hear. And as long as you don’t piss off your local stations.” Gil looked at Ahab, the man with grease on his hands. “You can make noise if that’s all you want.”

Ahab said nothing. He rubbed his hands on his pants, picked up a wrench, and tapped it on the sink, as if its rhythm was more interesting to him than the discussion.

“Let’s get back to print,” Gil challenged again, “something that can reach more than a two-block radius. Something that travels hand to hand. A sheet of paper’s still the most advanced communication form in the world. That’s why Liza’s here. Right, Liza?”

Liza looked down, touched her dress shyly, and smiled.

“You write history. I just want to make it.” Ahab was looking at Liza too, and instinctively she shaded her face with her hand. There was something behind Ahab’s gray eyes that pulsed like the channels of power he wanted to use. Something potent as a radio beam.

For several seconds, they all held their breath.

"Simple media is basic media," Rachel said, breaking the tension by siding with Gil.

The others laughed nervously.

"Forget about radio, equipment we don't have. A pamphlet is as simple as getting a typewriter," Rachel continued.

"I've got a typewriter," Liza offered.

It had been a long time since anyone had slept in the *Persephone*'s aft cabin, which was a narrow space with two bunks, a small sink, and a cabinet where Liza's father had stored his books on navigation. Liza suspected that some evenings her father, not wanting to come home after work, had stolen a few hours there reading or resting. The night of the meeting at Rachel's, it was a place to bring Gil.

The dock was quiet, the boat still. Through the porthole, she could make out a few lights, unwavering. She'd never been alone with a boy. Now she stood for a moment gazing at him. He was staring right back at her. Recklessly, she pulled her dress up over her head. He bent toward her and put his arms around her, unclipping her bra. "This is the last time we'll deal with that," he said, opening the porthole and flinging the bra out into the silvery water. She watched him pull off his own clothes.

"Turn around," he said, and she did, holding onto the edge of the bunk, where her father's body had left an impression in the old mattress. Gil had not kissed her.

He did not kiss her until afterward, when they lay in the musty bunk, hardly sleeping, and morning light filled the cabin. She didn't think about school or her mother's worry. She thought about pushing away from the dock for good and forever, and holding onto this sensation. She heard geese overhead and thought about the generator. For the first time since her father's death, she wanted to bring the sleeping boat to life. The body beside her was exciting to touch. In its nakedness. She ran a hand over it.

When she got home, three of her mother's friends were talking in the front room. She smiled at them, aware of her uncombed hair, and beat a retreat to the kitchen, where her mother was preparing a tray of tea. Her mother did not look up. "Take out the tray, will you?" she said. No mention of the night before. "Make sure you offer the milk first. I don't want my cups to crack."

Liza adjusted the teacups in their saucers, then placed the sugar bowl and creamer on the tray, lifting it carefully in both hands. After months of mourning, her mother was finally seeing friends again.

Longing to run upstairs and shut the door to her room, Liza poured the tea slowly after inquiring politely about sugar and milk. She nodded, smiled, said, "It's my pleasure," and "How is your little dog?" then set down the tray. Upstairs, she quickly packed a suitcase, taking only the rough clothes she would need for living on the boat. She took a bar of soap, three towels, checks for the bank account she'd opened after her father's death. She ran her hands along the spines of the books on her shelves—*The Tales of King Arthur, For Whom the Bell Tolls, War and Peace.*

In her father's study, she put his typewriter into its carrying case. Suitcase in one hand, typewriter in the other, a box of stiff, clean paper under her arm, two typewriter ribbons in her coat pocket, she went quietly out the back door.

For a week of nights, Gil came down to the boat to be with her. Sometimes it was the aft cabin, but more and more often they put a blanket on the deck in the galley near the stove, because it was warm. Awake all night, they slept when light began to seep into the cabin. Sometime after noon, Gil would pull on his clothes and make his way up the ladder. Liza would sleep again, waking as the sun was setting to make a pot of coffee and watch the last light leave the sky. She thought that she wasn't different from the way she had been before—it was just that she was learning to know her night self, a self that was darker and more interesting. When she thought of her school books, her gym clothes, the belongings packed away in her school locker, she decided that someone would cut the lock off and give everything away. She did not miss her mother, whose friends in the front room had somehow released Liza from the obligation of sharing grief. If it thrilled her to think her mother might come down to the boat one morning and find her there, naked, in the arms of this boy, she was unable to explain to herself why. She didn't ask herself what Gil did during the day, assuming his activities had something to do with the collective, as he called it, although he hadn't mentioned the newsletter or the typewriter that now sat on the chart table.

On the eighth day, as he was leaving, she said, "I want to help."

"You have school."

"It's almost out."

"All the more reason to go. You're a senior. Go ahead and graduate."

She watched him pulling on his boots, watched a margin of light push itself gently through the small porthole as if trying to join them. Putting out her hand, she reached to touch his back.

"Liza, listen. Don't try too hard."

She bit her lip and turned away.

"You're missing classes. Go on back. Get finished with that."

"What's the point?"

"You can't become a believer overnight." He glanced around, looking for softer words. "You might not be cut out for this life. It might be too rough and dirty for you."

"What's different about me?"

"We're going to stir things up. People like us are getting into tight groups and doing things that . . . we're trying to . . ." He took her hand and held it against his face, blinking. "What I'm saying is that maybe you have nothing in your life to fight against—no anger, no bruises. My old man's running an oil company. That's the bullshit I regard as my mortal foe."

Gil was right. She wasn't angry. Always she had been frozen, stopped. "You don't know what I am inside. Not really."

He moved her hand to his stomach. Tenderly she felt the familiarity of his skin. He said, "We can't keep you around just because we like you and you're a nice person to make love to, and then have you get tired or scared. What's going to happen next will be scary at the very least, and maybe illegal."

"I want to be with you." She amended this. "I want to be part of it."

"Don't do an action because you're stuck on a guy, Liza." They were lying on the bunk now, and he was pushing a boot off with his foot, undressing again.

For Liza, joining the collective was like learning the names of the ship's lines with her father, although she did not tell her new friends this. There was a process and she was moving through it, trying to understand how to march to a particular step, losing her ego, giving in to the will of the group. "Stop identifying with what you've been taught," Gil said gently. There was knowledge in him that Liza admired. She liked the way he tilted his head to one side when she asked him a question. He didn't answer too quickly.

Liza thought of her mother, even now plumping the pillows in their little house, tending her speckled irises and genealogy, keeping the calm exterior that had numbed Liza to her own life. Her mother seemed to be ringed in by fear of anything external, but maybe it was the internal self she would not acknowledge. Sometimes Liza thought of the inevitable moment when her mother would appear on the dock. She thought of what she would say to explain herself, afraid that her mother might deceive her into going home. But her mother never came.

One afternoon, Rachel and Pegasus came down to the harbor and called to her from the dock. Gil had gone off to meet someone, but they assured Liza that he had instructed them to come. "Rachel's old man is back,"

Pegasus announced, as if they were children whose secret clubhouse had been discovered in a back lot. Liza threw down the rope. Neither of them had ever been on a boat. They crossed the barrier of open space between the *Persephone*'s hull and the concrete dock, jolting the old boat as they jumped on deck.

That night, Gil said they should sail to Toledo, a city with lots of schools and community colleges, places where they could reach the ears and minds of students. Taking the boat would be easier than all of them hitch-hiking, and they'd have a place to sleep. But the *Persephone* was in no shape to leave the harbor. So while Gil read manuals, Liza showed Rachel and Pegasus how to replace rotten lines with new rope from a long spool. If Ahab had been there, the boat might have sailed sooner, but Ahab had disappeared.

Never having managed the *Persephone*'s great bulk on her own, Liza could not decide how to delegate responsibility. She could hear her father's lost voice in her ears, but shouting the drill to these people was impossible since the simplest command, such as "Ready about," would have to be explained. She would have to establish a hierarchy of command, but in truth Gil was usually the one who knew what they should do and where they should do it, so she would have to learn how to decode his ideas and then match the movements of the boat to his expectations. She would have to command her crew while taking orders, more or less. It might just be possible, because she was in love with this group of friends and with the man who fed them ideas. In love. It was a new idea to her.

Gil had chosen her. Everyone noticed. Each night, he

moved to her bunk and lay down beside her. In this way, he made it easy. They could lie together like that, without any discussion of what it meant or didn't mean. "Your bunk has just enough room for me," he said.

"This is my father's bed," she reminded him with a poke in the ribs. "Show a little respect! You have to call me captain when I'm on top."

They spent as much time laughing as anything else, which allowed her to understand how lonely she had been. And she had found a way to pleasure. "Having sex," Gil told her, "is bringing us closer. Or just call it fucking."

"You're afraid of your deep, intense side," she said, taking off his dark glasses and looking straight into his eyes.

"Am not. Don't have one."

She felt lovely. Loved. Felt her own hair and skin as translations of her exuberance. She wore fewer and brighter clothes. They were king and queen of this vessel, although the *Persephone* still hadn't left its berth.

Then Ahab came back. Buoyed up, actually bouncing, he seemed to be animated by a drug none of them had yet tried. It was early May. Liza and the others had been living as a group on the boat for two weeks. Ahab walked to the stern, then turned and headed toward the bow. Another abrupt turn. Back and forth, walking the length of the boat several times, as if the integrity of the vessel had to be tested. Liza watched his pacing with interest, imagining the ghost of her father walking beside this fierce, younger man. "Arrogant s.o.b.," her father would have said, as Ahab assumed an authority he hadn't earned.

"Let's get this beast moving," Ahab said, as if to the ghost. "Show me the engine first."

Liza led him below and into the engine room with an ambivalence that swung between rage and gratitude. Someone to work on the engine! He ran his hand over the cold metal block, then abruptly left her standing alone and returned with a roasting pan in one hand. He lay down, shimmying his body beneath the engine, and began draining the oil, working in silence, occasionally grunting. She did not know whether she should stay or leave him there. Her father had always wanted her company. "Read to me," he'd say, and she would read the newspaper to him while he puttered away under the engine, never explaining what he was doing. Why hadn't she asked? Had she imagined that he would always be there? Now she said, "Tell me what you're doing."

"Then come down."

She lowered herself to the deck boards and lay down beside him. With the oil draining, he'd begun dismantling the engine. "To grease it" was all he said.

Things about him conspired to make her nervous. Was it the tension just under the surface? He was older than the others, there was that. And he hardly acknowledged her. He didn't seem interested in anything but his own forward motion. She was cold. She wanted to move around or help him or get up and bring in an electric heater. But he had told her to lie down, and she didn't move.

Suddenly he spoke. "I worked a summer with your old man. I was sorry to hear when he died."

"Thanks." She was more troubled than surprised.

"I would've gone to the funeral, but . . ."

"There wasn't one," she offered, feeling exposed.

"So I heard."

"Actually, his ashes are here on the boat."

"That so?"

"I mean, maybe you can still come to the funeral." She couldn't remember now how she and her mother had justified this lack of a formal ceremony. Somehow, getting this engine working seemed like the first proper tribute she'd made to her father since his death.

"He helped me once," Ahab said quietly. "I almost poured liquid steel on myself. Your old man saw that it was going to happen." He told her then about the molten orange metal on the concrete floor of the plant, the screech of machines called to a halt, the foreman rushing across the cavernous room with sweat dripping off his face. "I could have lost my job, but your old man took it on and vouched for me all the way, said he'd stay with me till I got the feel—'got the knack,' that was how he put it."

Liza had never heard Ahab put so many words together, nor had she ever spoken to another man about her father. But he turned his attention back to the engine. "Oil and diesel," he said. "There's a place we can get them. Easy." His hands were black, the short, broken nails full of grease. As if he'd come to the boat straight from the steel plant. Steelers—what Gil always called boys from their town who were working class. She laughed a little.

He said, "I like the sound of that."

In the head, Liza was alone. *Bathroom*, the others called it, although she corrected them. A tiny cubicle, narrow at one end. Toilet. Mirror. Basin. Paper holder. An excuse for solitude. She sat with her face in her hands. Listening to her own breathing. The creak of the dock magnified by the steel hull. Gulls. Things unseen.

Finally they were ready for Toledo, which would be their first action as a collective. As they pulled away from the pier, the engine rumbling stoically, Liza was thrown into panic. It was one thing to live on the boat in the harbor, quite another to take it away without telling her mother.

Gil and Ahab loosened the lines from the dock. She was leaving everything in her life. Except the *Persephone*. Throwing the engine into gear, pushing them out of the harbor and into the lake's embrace, she put her head back, facing the sky, letting her long hair blow away from her shoulders in the rush of air. A hand slipped across her eyes—small, delicate. "You made all this happen," Rachel sang to her softly, moving her hand so that Liza could watch the horizon recede.

The town where Liza had grown up appeared as an outline, long and flat, unremarkable, just buildings against sky. She saw the trees that were only now beginning to fatten again, like herds let out to graze. In the summer, they shaded the hot streets. She remembered the long lassitude of childhood summers, the smell of mown grass and reedy lake, and the comradely feel of her father's nearness. She remembered the long-lost secret intensity of her time with Jolene.

"I wonder if any other girl has a boat like this," Rachel remarked.

"My father had to die first."

"Nobody dies too soon. If you know what I mean." Rachel put her arm around Liza's shoulders. She said,

"When we get to Toledo, stay close to me. I'm going to look out for you."

That night, a storm threw them into sudden darkness. They had eaten dinner, sitting loosely in a group on deck, and were gathering plates and spoons into piles afterward, when a hard wind blasted against the sails, sending dishes clattering across the planks, along with a pot of chili and the remains of a bowl of salad. Rachel grabbed at the pot, falling on her hands as a wall of water splashed over the deckhouse and swept spoons, forks, pots, and plates into the lake. Liza screamed, "Grab it!" and watched as Ahab dove for the red metal box that held her father's boat tools. She'd left the box unlatched, and now she saw the tools fly out of it and slide across the wet deck. Before Ahab could reach them, another wave hit, flicking the box away, as Gil, in water up to his knees, stumbled to the rail and grabbed for a cable. The boat righted itself, then pitched again, throwing him into the ratlines. *At sea, we never indulge a whim*: words of her father, whose ordinary tools were now lost.

When the *Persephone* righted itself again, Rachel handed Liza a crescent wrench, which seemed now to be an heirloom.

The group was on deck, shivering, huddled against the wind. Ahab shouted to Gil, "Up, man, come on!" They ran toward the bow, pulling themselves up the ratlines and shimmying along the metal stays that ran under the yardarm, and began to haul up and lash the square sails. The boat bobbed and plunged like a weightless matchbox, dipping the port yardarm so that Ahab, hanging there, was swallowed for an instant in the rising waves.

Liza watched him fight to maintain his footing. "Lash on!" she yelled. "Lash on!" Her voice was drowned in what seemed like rain but was the tops of waves, blown by the wind. She turned the ship like a battering ram into the wall of water, calling to the others to douse the headsails, which beat and strained against their tethers. Her friends weren't ready for this, they weren't trained. She could not read the compass that dipped and spun in its brass housing. *There's no point in steering*, she told herself, *just hold steady, will the ship on, will the bodies on board to stay put.*

Ahab, hold on.

All night, they took turns at the helm, with only the mainsail set—at half-mast—to steady them, a keel in air, while below in the depths, a red metal box slowly sank, hitting a rock, a sunken oil drum, the thick detritus of the lake's past, and came to rest, open as a hand, in the ancient mud. One by one, the silver tools followed—hammer, scraper, clamp—drifting, drifting down, never to be touched again.

When the sun rose in the morning, the wind slowed, and the sky blew clear enough for Liza to take their bearings and determine a course. Now the tired crew stripped off their wet clothing and hung shirts and shorts and underwear on the ratlines, throwing themselves down naked on the warm wood of the deck to look up at a thumbnail of moon against the blue, watching as another kind of front moved in across the cloudless sky. "Look!" A cloud of swallows was descending, darting and flickering, the blue V of their under-feathers visible from below. "How the hell'd they make it through that wind?" someone asked, as Rachel brought a pan of stale bread up on deck. Liza tore off a piece, holding it aloft, feeling the slight weight of a tired swallow perch for an instant on her hand.

In Toledo, a few of them visited the bookstore where Gil's friend from college worked. The place was crammed with second-hand records and books, old magazines, and vats of homemade tempeh. A kettle was roaring in the back. A cat lay in the window, sleepily braced by a cactus plant. Gil's friend, whose name was Carl, told them their timing was good. There was going be a protest against the Bank of America. "Rents," he said, without further details. He didn't give them the background, but the main idea, he said, was to "rile up the cops. That way people turn against them, people who never would otherwise."

While Carl talked, Ahab seemed not to be listening. He strolled to the front window and leaned over to scratch the cat's ear.

"You went to college?" Liza said to Gil.

"Yale," he said. "Only lasted two years."

"Why'd you go back to Erie?"

"Ask Ahab." Gil nudged her.

Ahab looked up laconically. "Someone had to take the Midwest." He came back to the small group, grabbed Gil from behind, and closed an arm around his neck, as if to choke him.

Gil laughed, twisted out of Ahab's grip. "Oh, come back to me, come back . . . That's what he said to me."

So Ahab and Gil had known each other long before the rest of the group had come together. "How long?" Liza asked.

"Since he saw a bunch of steelers kicking the shit out of me," Gil answered, "and saved my righteous ass."

A sign over the cash register said, ANTI-IMPERIALIST TEXTS and FIND THE REVOLUTION HERE!! A North Vietnamese flag flew over the bathroom door.

"Everyone's coming at eight," Carl told them. "We're thinking the pigs know what we're up to—so be ready."

Under her breath, Liza asked Rachel how the police could know.

"Shoes," Rachel said.

Liza smiled, looked away, but Rachel explained anyway. "Undercover FBI. Even you could be one. You have to suspect everybody."

From various piles on the floor of the store, Gil picked up copies of *New Left Notes*, *Ramparts*, *Rat*. Carl had a mimeograph machine at the back of the store and gave them each a stack of pamphlets to hand out at the protest. On the boat, they made themselves ready, putting on layers of clothing, their heaviest shoes.

"We need helmets," Gil pointed out.

Ahab disappeared, presumably to find helmets, but he came back later saying they would have to do without.

"Little brains could get busted," Pegasus joked, as they made their way out of the Toledo harbor and through the city, street lights coming on, doors closing for the night.

Liza sniffed at the warm air of spring and felt a gush of fellowship as they rounded a corner to see a small crowd gathered in a muddy park. Children and adults were sitting on spread blankets. A dozen guitars played at once and loudspeakers had been set up, as if they were going to dance. There were signs, balloons, banners, and a papier mâché puppet on a pole. A boy, ten or eleven years old, ran through the park wearing a blanket around his shoulders like a cape. Some students had set up a table under a street light. They were collecting names on a petition. Why would anyone think they needed helmets? Rachel poked Liza from behind and pointed to a brown Oldsmobile pulled up to the curb near the students' table. "Shoes. We should've worn masks. Don't get photographed."

Gil came up behind her. "Ready to go? Open your pocket." She did, and he poured a handful of sand into it. Now he took her by the arm and they set off together through the mud and across the lot to the students' table. She noticed Ahab follow and then sprint toward the brown car. Throwing both hands on it, he swung his body up, stomping up and down on the hood, then jumping onto the roof. Two men got out of the car, and Gil leapt at the one on the driver's side, flinging a handful of sand at the man's eyes. Liza ran after the other man, but he dodged her and made off down an alley. Cops were converging from different directions with clubs in their hands and helmets on their heads, but before they reached Liza, a group of people got in the way, blocking them, and suddenly the park was chaos, music blaring from the loudspeakers. She heard a *crack*, loud and explosive, from the direction of the bank. Gil?

Rachel was there. They were running, Rachel and Gil. Liza saw them spin and dash out of the park, Rachel slipping once and Gil pulling her up. Standing still, Liza wondered where to go, what to do next. Entirely alone now, while people pushed against her, she heard nothing but silence, watching from a distance as signs tore in the night breeze, balloons burst, children ran back into mothers' arms, fathers and comrades dispersed.

Gil and Rachel were far ahead.

She followed.

On the *Persephone*, when she saw that her cabin door was shut, she did not try to open it, but took a blanket up to the forward cabin, near the galley, where Ahab and Pegasus usually slept. "Was I wrong for expecting him to be faithful?"

"Ownership is what he works against," Pegasus said, offering a little irony, but then, because she had disappointed him, he got up and left the galley.

She found an empty bunk and crawled in, thinking of the brown Oldsmobile and the two men, like scared dogs, ducking out of it, thinking of the sand in her pocket, in the air, of the man with his fists up wiping at his eyes. She heard the hatch slide back and heavy footsteps on the ladder. Soon the galley lamp was lit. Ahab stood at the sink and opened his coat, pulling something out of it. He wrapped the object in a cloth and stashed it above the stove. Then he turned on the sink taps, using the foot pedal to pump water on his hands, and splashed his face. He took off his clothes. "If you prefer modesty, I can turn off the light."

"I prefer to watch." She wanted to be back in her cabin where Gil was, but she liked the way her words surprised Ahab.

He turned back to his pile of clothes and took something

else out of his coat. He moved his hands over it, put it to his mouth, and began playing a strange little tune. When he stopped, he said, "How does a ship sail into the wind?"

She sat up on her bunk. "Come here."

"You're going to demonstrate?"

"I want to know if you always do what you're told."

"That depends."

"On what?"

"Maybe on who or what it serves." He sat down on the edge of the bunk and fingered the recorder.

"I mean, the group, sharing, doing what we're told. What if they told you to sleep with me?" she said.

With the other hand he pressed her against the bunk. "Only in the line of duty."

"And what if they tried to stop you?"

He lifted her blanket, as if he already knew her skin under the denim shirt, the weight of her silver bracelets, her wild hair.

"Theoretically, I mean." She felt his hand move down to her breast. She did not like his hands; they were ugly, rough. They had worked in her father's plant. "Don't," she said. But it was too late.

They sailed, purposefully, between the towns on Lake Erie. At night, they folded down the bunks in the main cabin, which was separated from the galley by a long steel counter, and sat around the small collapsible table. There was food and argument. The food was always cooked in one pot. The argument was always about the connection between their work and the work of the Black Panthers. Gil, who drew more sustenance from the stash of marijuana he carried around than from the food on his plate, rolled joints and inhaled, sucking in as he talked. "We're the same as black Americans," he said. "We're young. We're fucked by the system." He talked about the way the system had robbed the black man of his dignity. "We can't be Black Panthers, but we can sure as hell be with them."

Liza thought of Jolene.

Seated at the galley table, her dinner half finished, she suddenly spoke. "The lakes are a vein running through everything. We're mobile. More than anybody else, we can go from one place to another."

All of them looked at her. Gil made a snoring sound. Rachel laughed softly. Ahab said nothing, as usual. Only Pegasus replied. "Wherever the wind goes," he said. "Skull and crossbones shall be our flag."

Liza felt the blood move in each part of her body; she was no longer connected to herself. It was summer now and most nights they slept on deck. Sometimes she lay beside Gil and sometimes Rachel did. She told herself it didn't matter. The stars were charging her to act.

The first time they went back to Erie, Liza got on a bus. The idea came to her all at once.

"What's your plan?" Gil asked. "You've got your shoes on. Your purse. You off to town, Mrs. Brown?"

"Nothing. Just an idea."

"Can I come?"

"I'm not even sure where I'm going."

She took him not to her old neighborhood but to a street she had seen only once: a street with small houses, sagging porches, cracked sidewalks, a street on which everything seemed to need either water or paint, except for the empty lot where Jolene's house had stood.

Liza could see it from the corner when she and Gil stepped off the bus. "I had a friend who used to live here," she explained, because Gil had come along without asking any questions. "She used to sail on the boat," she added inconsequentially, as the bus wheezed off, lumbering up the quiet street. Gil touched her arm, then thought better of it as she stood waiting. Not for Jolene. She had never seen Jolene in this place. She was waiting for an inspiration, waiting for grief. The loss of the only person who had ever made her feel brave. Until she'd met Gil. So it seemed appropriate that he had come—maybe she owed Jolene at least this introduction. She had not mourned her father, who had died so suddenly of a heart attack. She had not thought about her mother's distress at a husband's death and a daughter's abandonment. She hadn't cared about unfinished exams or the rebellious life she was openly leading. And somewhere, in this heady experiment, she had almost forgotten Jolene. Why had she let herself do that? Oh, Jolene! With Gil, Liza stood on the ruined ground of the vacant lot where the house had burned, pushing hair off her face.

"Hot, isn't it. Nice of you to come." Liza stood, looked down at the sun-dried grass. "She died when this house burned down, and then I had to go on the boat every weekend with just my father. Week after week, all summer long. Month after month. Even in the fall and spring. I got sick of it, truly. It was torture, but I couldn't say that to him. He was trying so hard to be nice and take my mind off my friend, and all I wanted to do was hang out with other kids, people my own age, boys. I wasn't thinking that much about Jolene. It was like a glitch. Do you know what I mean? I wanted to be normal."

Gil rubbed her hand.

As they stood there, an old man emerged from the bushes that circled the house next door. Perhaps he had seen them through the window. "Po' gal," he said, and Liza thought he must mean Jolene. He said the words so tentatively, and with such a lisp, that she asked, "Did you know them?"

He shook his head. "Bosses did it, what I heard."

Liza stared at the overgrown clumps of weeds and grass that covered what had once been a yard. Right on this street, the Cadillac had sat, its engine idling. And all of them in it, her mother, her father, herself. All she wanted at this minute was to bring back her friend, carry her to the boat, tend to her wounds.

"Her daddy was the union man."

Gil said, "Is that right?" As if he meant to stay and converse, but Liza did not want him to take charge of this moment.

Waiting for the return bus, she forced herself to think of the times Al Shore and his daughter must have waited for it to take them to the harbor, the times she and her own father might have picked them up in the car. For some reason, this thought, forming itself into regret, stuck in her mind. She would always see the ugly ground and the intrepid weeds and grass, and she would never forget the smell of the burned wood, linoleum, and tar that hung impossibly around the vacant lot after so much time. But it was the wheezing bus that angered her. *Po' gal.*

At the boat, Ahab was jubilant. "I got it, man, I got it. Enough cash to keep us for six weeks!"

Pegasus was hunched over the table, and seemed to be laughing.

Gil pointed at Pegasus. "What happened?"

Ahab shrugged, lifting a fist. "Nothing. No big deal." They were below deck, the *Persephone* enfolding them. "It was a bank. Just one guard. We got in and out in ten minutes." He let out a whoop.

Gil smiled, putting a hand on Pegasus' shoulder. "Don't worry about it. It'll pass."

It was clear to Liza now that Pegasus was crouched over in distress, that his usual good humor had vanished. He said something no one could hear. The boat rose and fell on the swells of the lake.

"Bound to be a security guard at a bank. Pegasus let it get to him."

"I wasn't expecting a gun, that's why." Pegasus let each word out slowly.

Gil said, "What gun?"

But Ahab was ahead of Gil. "Shit, man. You think I'd walk you in there unarmed?"

Gil, who chose this moment to go to the sink, put his head under the faucet and turned his mouth to it for a long drink, listened carefully, then straightened himself. He looked at Ahab for a long moment, then turned back to the sink, pumping the water until it spilled over the draining board onto the galley's deck.

No one spoke.

Rachel stood up and moved around the table to Gil, turning off the tap.

Gil stopped pumping.

Ahab said, "I only pointed it at the guard," in a tone that sounded defensive.

Gil considered this, and then said, "I guess we have a lot to thank our friends for. Taking this risk in order to put food on our table." Water still dripped off the counter around his feet.

Ahab crossed the small space between them and got down on his knees to mop up the water with a cloth.

"And we appreciate," Gil went on, "your generous impulse, leaving us out of the equation to spare us, I'm sure, even after we agreed to act as a group here, assuming that this whole summer was about collective action and not personal heroics, which is why we appreciate so much your taking all this danger onto yourself."

"You're welcome," Ahab said, and now he went to the chair Rachel had left. He sat down next to Liza, who remained unmoving. She did not like having a gun on the boat, but she had known it was there, had seen him put it away, and hadn't told anyone about it, even Gil. She had turned away from the sight of it and taken this man into her arms for reasons that were too complex to consider. She kept her eyes on Gil, but felt Ahab beside her.

In Erie, a new person got on the boat. She was a friend of Pegasus', she said. "Where is he?" Standing on the dock, her head tilted back, staring up at Liza and Rachel who were scrubbing the aft decks, she looked young and forlorn.

"Don't know," Rachel said. "They went off this morning." Rachel was not going to tell anyone anything. Neither was Liza.

"I'm Joyce," she said, sticking her hand up.

Liza stopped scrubbing long enough to take the hand and shake it. "Come on aboard."

Over coffee, they learned that Pegasus' father had had a long affair with Joyce's mother. "We put it together. On the nights his dad said he had to work, my mom happened to be out. So Peg and I started doing it too. It was his idea, kind of a joke on his old man. You know, I even gave Pegasus his name—a horse with wings, that's the size and shape of it." She laughed. "I brought him a present, but I'll share it with you. To make friends." She pulled out a tab of acid. Liza and Rachel looked at it. Was it selfish to do the acid without the others? Especially when they were off stealing more diesel.

"Let's go," Rachel said.

Joyce took off her glasses, folding them neatly and setting them down on the table. Liza noticed how pretty Joyce was—little nose and little lips, a tiny mole on her chin. She watched as Joyce broke the tab with her fingernail, handing a piece to each of them. Liza swallowed hers.

It was hot in the cabin. The summer sun burned down on the steel hull, heating the inside like a pot coming to a boil.

"Maybe we should lie down." Joyce stretched across one of the bunks. While they waited for the acid to hit, she said, "There's gonna be a big action in Chicago in October."

Lying between Rachel and Joyce, Liza rolled over and looked at Joyce's face, the eyes deeper and colder than any she had ever seen. Something was moving Joyce's mouth. Liza watched the tiny mole on Joyce's chin dance like a star adrift from its constellation. She saw that Rachel's mouth was touching Joyce's mouth. A green happiness filled her, a bulb shooting out of tight earth. She beheld the movement of mouths, arms, hands, air moving through the cabin. It was the same air that fed the speckled iris. Air that filled the sails. Air that moved between Joyce's lips when she spoke. Liza knew it did not matter who lay down beside whom. She could let go of all the cards she'd been holding so tightly to her chest and show them to everyone. All the cards were the same card. A horse with wings. It was the green air that told her this.

A PEAR TREE,
A BOX OF DYNAMITE

Yonge Street was crowded with shoppers. Mark pushed past three musicians, noticing the snow falling into their open instrument cases. One saxophone, two guitars. All playing different songs only a few feet apart. He remembered a word Faye had taught him and his mood lifted. *Cacophony.* He wanted to stand in the snow that glowed beneath the lights, watching fingers move across the strings, watching the pressure on the instrument that strained the strap around the guitarist's neck and the flick of tension at the wrist when the instrument was lifted to meet the fingers on a particularly complicated riff. It thrilled him that the guitarists weren't listening to each other, that they stood inside their own music. He wanted to linger with them, teasing apart their separate songs, but he had already burned all his matches along with the better part of daylight, and he knew, somewhere in the back of his mind, that Faye needed him to move quickly. Mere had never spent a night away from the boat before. Whatever was happening to them was as tangled up and complicated as the cacophony of noises on the street.

He stopped at a hot dog cart to savor the smell and look at the jars of condiments lined up on a metal shelf under the umbrella. An old man in a wheelchair pushed against him. "You next in line or me?"

"No. Help yourself." Mark could not afford a hot dog, but enjoyed his own generosity, moving aside and even offering to help the seated man by pushing him under the cart's umbrella.

"I'll take a sausage dog. Could you reach behind me in the bag and get out my wallet?"

Mark took the required money from the wallet and handed it to the hot dog man, who held out the sausage in a well-toasted bun, but Faye had told Mark not to touch food after handling money. "Could you please pass it down to him?" he asked the hot dog man.

"Why don't you push your friend away, pal?"

Mark gripped the handles of the chair and pushed it toward the crosswalk. The light turned and he shoved the chair into the street, through the accumulating slush. It was hard work, and Mark, who liked to feel the blood moving in his muscles, felt completely awake for the first time all day. Up on the sidewalk, he noticed people moving out of the way. Some smiled at him, others stared, a few just looked down. Once behind the man, Mark had a chance to study the ragged cap on the head, the stained Maple Leafs jacket that rode up over the belly. *Maple Leaves,* Mark thought absently, hearing Faye's voice in his head. The man wore a pair of corduroy pants, ragged at the cuffs where his feet—one in a boot and one wrapped in gauze bandages—perched on the metal footrests. The man's fly was unzipped.

What would Faye think of him now?

He could never do things right where she was concerned. The time they had lost the anchor, and he had gone into the lake carrying a long line lashed to the deck. He'd swum into the blackest water, holding his breath and closing his eyes—they were no help in the dark—and feeling with his hands for the bottom. Twice he'd had to go up for air, but the third time he'd felt the floor of the lake, reaching out, touching rocks, his chest bursting, forehead pounding with the cold and the pressure, his lungs on fire. He'd fumbled for the metal flukes of the anchor. Then his hands found the metal eye, and with the last of himself, he tied the rope through it, pushing off the bottom, breaking through the surface to air. On deck, he'd felt triumphant, but Faye did not blink. "You tied it properly, I hope." And when they couldn't heave up the anchor, he'd gone back down, following the rope carefully, hand over hand, to move whatever rocks were weighing down the flukes. A rock had rolled onto his hand, but when he came out of the water, shouting that he'd broken his finger, Faye had offered him a brandy instead of a doctor, managing in this way to remind him that he was an outcast, in spite of the anchor, in spite of everything.

✦

A cage ran the length of the room in Merril's basement. Inside it, dozens of birds. "My hyacinth macaws," he said to Mere proudly. A blur of blue and red wings, little claws hanging onto wires, beaks and tufted head feathers. "My pride and joy. They're getting scarce."

"Like endangered," Mere said, trying to impress. One of the birds was making a noise like the sound of rigging on a windy night. "How did you get them?" she asked.

"From eggs." He shrugged. "They're birds."

She saw that he hadn't understood her, and remembered the paper she'd read in his study.

"Do you sell them?"

"You have to sell something if you want to buy something. That's the nature of life, sweetie," he said, using his first endearment. "Anyway, don't you think birds and wild animals want a nice place to live, like Rogue?"

"They already live in nice places." She sounded barely petulant, testing out on him the voice she used with her mother.

"But the macaws I sell just come from eggs. I mean, they wouldn't miss the forest because they've never seen it." He gave her arm a sharp tap, as if requiring her to think realistically. "If I don't put them in a cage, they'll all die out. At the rate the forests are getting chopped down, guys like me are the ones who save wild animals. With birds, you have to work hard to get them to breed, and that's what it's all about—the breeding, interbreeding, improving the breeds." He was off now, talking about things Mere might have been interested in, but not here, not right now, not when she was trying to know this man and have him know her. "It's hard getting eggs to hatch. It takes light, the right amount of heat, and even a certain amount of moisture, and of course the egg has to be fertilized at the exact right moment." He stopped himself, noticing at last that she wasn't listening. She had moved a step closer to the cage. "Do you want to hold one?" he asked.

She hesitated. "Maybe. Okay."

He took the clip out of the gate and reached his hand into the cage. One of the birds jumped onto it. "This is Rosie," he said, and lowered the bird onto her arm.

"But she's blue."

He looked at Mere blankly.

The bird moved up her arm, reaching its beak to her ear. Suddenly the bird was in her hair. Panicked, she shook her head, but its claws were in her scalp, and she tried to knock it off with her hands.

Merril stopped her. "Jesus Christ, you could hurt her." He pulled the bird off, smoothing its feathers, setting it down on top of the cage, then he smoothed Mere's hair in the same way.

That afternoon Ellie and Merril left together. "Don't answer the door and don't talk on the phone," Merril instructed. "We won't be long. Take care of things."

Who would she call on the phone? Mere stepped outside into the snowy garden, finding the scent of dying flowers pleasantly foreign. Merril had mentioned the rule about not going outside this morning, but had not repeated it before he left. Walking deeper into the garden, she thought of the fence as a new and different boundary, her father's fence, the tall arched gate with its iron latch, a boundary she was not allowed to cross. Take care of things, he had said. The house was hers for the moment, and she felt lifted by that.

Rogue had come loose from his mooring. *Strange*, she thought, *I made him fast*. But he was still in the garden, her father's fence, a boundary for him too. *Take care of things.* She stood in the new-falling snow under the burdened branches of a pear tree, and in the cold air of November everything was redeemed: the secret meeting with her father, the forbidden ride in the taxi, the escape she had made without Faye's knowledge. She could see, as she walked through the garden with its sturdy flowers and frosted grass, that any steps taken on land left indelible marks, whereas all she'd ever left behind in her watery life was a furrowed wake that quickly disappeared. Life on the water did not have such consequence.

Under the tree, the grass was long and wet with snow that clumped in patches. It wet her sneakers and the bottom of her jeans, but Mere liked the cavern that the branches made, and she stood under them, looking up. A few feet above her head hung a withered pear, and she struggled to reach it, grabbing hold of the lower branches like ratlines. The pear came off in her hand. She bit into the autumn fruit, but it was dry and tasteless. Still, she would consume it because it was hers; she had discovered it. After a few more mealy bites, she threw it down in the soggy grass because there was no one to notice that she had not finished it.

She had never picked a piece of fruit before, except for some berries on Wolfe Island with Mark. That was not so long ago, but she could not remember their taste. It was before Mark had taken her up to the shack and before they had lain down together on the wooden floor under the swallows' nests. Before he had put his hand under her T-shirt and laid it warm and calloused on her heart.

On Wolfe Island, they had picked blueberries and walked from one end to the other as if they were on a different boat that had been wrecked in the shallows and grown over with weeds. Mark had found an old bone. He'd run after Mere for a while trying to scare her with it, saying it was part of a finger, then a penis, even though it was just an old rabbit bone that meant nothing. It was then she'd decided that what she wanted was to live on a farm. Sheep. Chickens. Cows. Horses. Goats. And Faye would like a farm after she got used to it. In the summer, she could sail around the lake when she wanted to, but in the winter, they would keep her busy at home making cheese out of goat's milk. They would have to get all the animals in and out of the barn. She and Mark would take care of Faye and the animals.

When Mere came out from under the branches of the tree in Merril's garden, she noticed a shadow moving near the gate. She was going to turn back to the house, but instead she went to see what the shadow was. *What's the point of this jump to land*, she was thinking, *if I can't open gates?* All of a sudden, she saw a hand between the slats. Mark!

"Oh," she said, as if caught in a forbidden act, and took a deep breath. "You came all the way here!"

Mark rattled the gate. "Let me in," he said, then stepped into the light, where she could see the expression on his face. He was a little irritated, as if she had put up this barrier on purpose. "Hey," he said, with the voice she knew better than anyone else's, all the modulations and catches. She had studied them, even practiced them. "Lemme in. C'mon. Let's get out of here. Faye's a wreck."

"How'd you do it?"

"Walked most of the way." He'd worked open the latch and was inside the garden. "Till a guy in a wheelchair explained about the subway. Come on, I'll show you on the way back."

"Subway?" Mere said, then quickly, "I know what I'm doing. This is my father's house." She walked to the pear tree and he followed.

"How can you be so sure? Faye didn't say that."

"There's nobody here. I could show you the whole place. There are birds in the basement called hyacinth macaws. Lots of them. And they're endangered. And he lifts weights and there are four TVs."

Mark said, "Who cares?" and Mere saw that she had hurt him. Now she wanted to make light of the house, but Mark said, "Do you know how bad you made Faye feel? She's probably going to be pumping the bilge by the time we get back!"

Mere clenched her fists. "This is my father's house and she never said a word about him. He's not bad. He could even have helped us out. That's what he says. He's going to talk to Faye about seeing me more." She had made this up, but found it believable. "Faye can come up and get me herself if she's so upset."

Mark made a scoffing sound. "She can't come here, you know that," he said impatiently. "There are reasons why she never goes on land, whatever they are."

"Can't she bend the rules just once to come visit her daughter?" Mere crouched down, ignoring the wet grass. "Maybe she'd like to see the kind of rooms they have here, even the bed. There's a living room, Mark. For nothing.

Just with the nicest furniture they have and one of the TVs. Why is it Faye never thought we should live in a house? Why is this so much more than she ever thought I should have?"

"She wants you to have what you need," Mark said softly. He sat himself down in the long, wet grass and stared at it, mashing it flat with the sides of his sneakers, taking a cigarette out of his pocket but not lighting it. "So what about me?" he asked.

She put her hand out and touched the sleeve of his jacket, but she couldn't think of anything to say.

✦

Faye stepped on the well-stubbed cigarette butt a final time and cast a long look at the radio towers. No wind at all. Snow hovered over the lake like a mist, pulling sky around her, socked in, horizonless.

On the boat, she could be trapped. But the children were coming. Surely they were. She could gather their belongings before they arrived. Take the chance now instead of later.

She opened Mere's locker first. Winter boots. Down-filled jacket. The pouch with acne soap, face cream, an almost untouched pink lipstick. Her daughter . . . was about to be thirteen. Child in the body of an adolescent. Child with budding breasts. A hint of waist and hips. On a pile of sweatshirts was the diary Mere called her dilemmas book or some such thing.

She should pack separate bags for the two of them—

and with this thought, she straightened up and took a quick look around. Surely there were other bags. Or she could put Mere's clothes in a pillowcase.

She grabbed a pillow from one of the bunks, pulling it out of the case, and a few feathers flew out. *The chickens*, she thought. Mere would have to lose the only pets she'd ever had. How would the land-world treat Mere? Long, dark months on the run would change her in so many ways. Faye felt through the locker for anything more her daughter might miss. She pulled out a sweater, and something hard, heavy, rolled out at her feet.

At a glance, she knew exactly what it was. Knew precisely the day it had been carried aboard. But when, how had Mere found it? It looked like a clock. Was a clock. Except that it wasn't.

Now, quite suddenly, Faye understood that Mere had gone with Merril through some plan of her own devising. All her talk of living on land, of having a farm and animals; all the begging for shore leave, had been for this. A father. What was the clock, if not a sign of Mere's devotion to the idea of him? She must have found this round lump of brass a long time ago.

Faye picked up the clock, remembering the day she had been released from police custody, had come back to the *Persephone* to find the others crouched over blasting caps, wires, and a box, the smell of which made her head ache.

Now she walked up the ladder to the stern of the ship, flinging the clock into the water, watching it glint as it sank to the bottom of Lighthouse Cove.

It was so hot in Detroit that the dogs of the city lay panting unhappily in any available shade. Someone had released a fire hydrant so that children could bear to play. In the early afternoon, carrying a red flag and distributing leaflets, Liza, Rachel, and Joyce marched into a crowded park. An all-women's action against the war. It had been Liza's idea. "Come to Chicago in October," Liza urged, holding up her arms as if the motley crowd could be persuaded by gesture. A few people passing by stopped to listen. They stood under the shade trees, and when they stayed long enough to get tired, they crouched down, as if not to miss a word. At this, Liza grew more eloquent. "We want to help you understand. Who ever tells you the truth anymore? Listen! I've come all the way here from Erie, Pennsylvania. I came here because I want to tell you what's going so wrong with this country around you." The crowd was growing. "Remember who is dying in Vietnam! They're people like you! Workers like you. And who's getting sent over there to kill them? Not the college boys!" Her arms above her head! Her newfound voice! "Help us fight this unholy system!" *Unholy*—she liked the sound of the word.

Later, when the sun seemed ready to roast them alive, they walked to a junior college in a neighborhood of auto workers. Here, Liza lifted her arms again, clenched her fists, and shouted to the students who lay like the city dogs, panting and weary on a few sorry patches of grass. "What are they training you for? They're training you to keep the black people down, the black people who are worse off than you! They're training you to maintain the status quo! And most of all, they're training you to support the war in Vietnam where women and children are being killed."

Where had the words come from? Joyce signaled to her, and the three of them ran into a nearby building where summer classes were taking place. There was a long hall and a line of closed doors. Joyce grabbed a knob and they burst in. Before anyone knew what was happening, they'd dragged the teacher's long desk in front of the door. The teacher was another woman, and obviously distressed. Ignoring her, Liza began to feel the strange excitement that had overtaken her when she'd been a student seated in a classroom a few months before. But how distant she now felt from these complacent students sitting in front of her. Though the teacher was barely older than she was, Liza felt nothing for her. "Come to Chicago in October! Help us fight racism, imperialism! An unjust war!"

Joyce shouted, "And the oppression of women!" It was a wholly new rallying cry.

The teacher ran to the open window, screaming out to the street, and Liza came up behind her, spinning the woman around, pinning her arms behind her back and pressing her up against the cinder-block wall. "You should be ashamed of yourself!" the teacher hissed. Liza froze for a second, but she regained her grip, now twisting the woman's arms and smelling her frightened breath.

Two boys stood up, pushed toward Liza, grabbing at her arms and hair. Other students were holding Joyce and Rachel. One of them, a boy with pointed teeth, demanded that they leave the classroom. "Go back to your freak friends!" the sharp-toothed boy hissed at Liza. "You pathetic ugly dyke!"

Liza slapped at him, and he pulled her to the floor. She felt only rage, no passivity, no fear. Someone kicked her hard in the ribs. "They're girls, stop beating up on them!" she heard, and "They asked for it." Two security guards pushed their way into the room. She felt the boy's weight and heat. She was aware of his acrid smell and of his hip bones, which were pressing against her own hips as if they were locked in a labor of love instead of hate. And why should he hate her? He had his hand on her face, and as hard as she could, she bit it, twisting her head to bring her teeth to his flesh. "Christ! Bitch!" He reared up then and hit her hard, as hard as he could, but his hand was something terrible; she had bitten through to the bone, and now she spit out the taste of his blood.

When the boy got to his knees and then stumbled off, Rachel and Joyce lay down beside Liza, putting their arms around her, refusing to leave the room, forcing the guards to drag them out. Unceremoniously they were pulled by their legs through the door and down the hall. It was the sensation of cold tile under skin that Liza remembered, and moving involuntarily, feet first, her head dragging behind. "Like a breech birth," Rachel said later.

They were propped up and shoved through the doors of the building onto the steps, which were too hot to be touched. From those steps, they were thrown into a police car, packed tight in the back seat behind a grid of wire mesh.

"Ma?" Liza was on the pay phone. "Ma?" Her voice was odd; she could hear that herself. The cop standing next to her didn't help. He could hear every word, was probably writing down every word or, worse, taping her phone call. That's what they did. "Well, I'm on the boat," Liza continued bravely, having only the faintest clue what she expected her mother to say or do. "Did you know?"

"No." Her mother's voice was strangely cold. It might have been rage or hurt, but it wasn't concern. Liza could not detect a shred of relief.

"I'm with friends from school." Liza wondered if her mother would believe this. She had kept hidden her lack of friends for so long that it was possible her mother would be convinced. "Friends you never met," she said in a rush, "but everyone decided to take the summer off and sail, and I was just so tired after exams—it all caught up with me . . . So we got the *Persephone* running without too much trouble. I tried to call and talk to you." She was lying, but she liked the sound of it.

Here, her mother laughed. She said, almost lightly, "But you didn't."

"I wanted you to know what I was doing, Mom, but I thought you'd be mad at me, and then it got harder." From where she stood in the hallway, Liza could see Rachel and Joyce in the small cell. They were sitting on the single cot, or rather one was sitting and one was lying down. Was Joyce really asleep? Liza was speaking softly, but her friends would hear everything, and they would probably think that she was sorry she'd ever joined up with them and was afraid to take the consequences. Joyce and Rachel were used to this kind of trouble. They had both been arrested once in the past. Now Liza said, "I know you've been worried to death. But I've been okay," and waited for her mother's response, but there wasn't any. What had she expected her mother to do: get in the car and drive to Detroit? *And if she asks me to come home, will I come home?* Liza didn't know. "I've been fine. I'm in Detroit." After the phone call, she would be put back in the cell. Four feet square. Back and forth. Back and forth.

At last her mother said, "Detroit." And then, "Why?"

"Because." She wound the telephone cord around her hand and pulled it tight, looking at Rachel again, whose eyes were locked shut. Rachel, whose mouth was a hard, thin line. "It's not serious at all. But we were doing a minor kind of demonstration and it got broken up." Liza stopped. She could hear her mother's short breaths but they did not tell her how to speak next. "Are you there, Ma?"

"Yes, of course."

"Are you okay?"

"I'm just fine, Liza Jane." Only when her mother was displeased did she use both of Liza's names.

Was the cell any different from her mother's living room? Yes, Liza had to admit it was. She would rather serve infinite cups of tea than walk back and forth across four feet of cell floor. But even so, there was honor in what she'd done. "It was a completely passive demonstration," Liza said. No honor in a porcelain teacup.

She had been playing at revolution, it was clear to her now—knowing she would always go home if her mother asked. This was why she hadn't given her mother an opportunity. But now, telephoning from the jail, she had. And her mother hadn't asked. Hadn't even asked where Liza might be going. Liza hung up the phone.

Gil and Ahab were crouched on the galley floor when Liza and the others clambered on board.

"Where the hell have you been?" Gil was fierce.

"We got busted," Joyce countered. There was pride in her voice.

"We're all gonna get busted, and for something worse than a protest if we don't get out of here." With that, Ahab walked off.

Gil spat out at them, "Don't touch a single thing," then turned and climbed up the ladder to the deck.

Footsteps overhead told Liza that Gil and Ahab were preparing to leave. A loud bell sounded from the engine room, and then the engine throbbed to life.

"We can't take off," Liza said to Joyce. "What about the court date?"

Joyce shook her head. "I'm not hanging around."

"Disorderly conduct. We can't just ignore it." Her head above her right eye had been throbbing since the cops dragged her down the hall. Her ribs were so sore, she could not bend or stretch. Now the noise of the engine gripped her as if her whole head were in a vise. And there was something else. "Do you smell something?" She had to scream to be heard over the engine.

She held her nose and looked at Joyce and Rachel quizzically. Did they smell something, sweet like ether, but heavier and bitter-tinged? She felt the boat slip its tethers and jerk into gear. The outside world slid past—nothing in her was strong enough to stop it. She walked forward to where the smell was even stronger and opened the bulkhead to the far forward cabin. A wooden box sat shoved against the bulkhead. DANGER. HIGHLY EXPLOSIVE.

Madness. In the summer heat, on board the boat, where if it exploded they would all be blown out of the water? Even with the whine and pressure in her head, Liza knew clearly that Gil and Ahab had lost their minds.

The two of them stood together at the helm. Gloating, she supposed. "When did you decide it was okay to bring dynamite on the boat?" She was angry now, and challenging both of them. "When?" Had they done this because Liza, Rachel, and Joyce had asserted themselves with their all-women protest?

"We didn't want to put you at risk by bringing you in on it."

"Well, I'm in now." Her tone was bitter. "And I want it off the boat. It's hot enough to explode."

"Clear a space in the fridge then, and we'll put it in there."

"If you had ever cooked a meal, you would know—" She stopped herself. What good would it do to tell them that they would have to run the generator day and night to keep the fridge cold enough? It was too late. They would have to do just that. There was no point in arguing because it was clear to her that she had to live on this boat, that she had no other home.

"Come here." Gil pulled at her until she was beside him at the helm. They stood holding it together, both facing the bow, their backs to Detroit. "This is only the beginning."

"That's good. I'm glad," she said, and after she said it, she realized that she meant it. If she could not go back to her mother, she wanted what she did to matter. Charged by the stars to act, she would act.

Later, when she went below, she would look through the old issues of *Ramparts*, find that ad for the lawyer, memorize his name, memorize his phone number. She would make sure Gil and the others did the same. They weren't playing anymore. Next time, if they were caught, the charges would be more serious.

Two weeks after Detroit, the *Persephone* nosed into the great bowl of Lake Michigan where the shore grew low and sandy, sloping gradually to the water without feature or incident. Liza could feel the difference—a great weight of water under the boat and the momentum of their course (set by Ahab) direct and southward, past sand hills formed by the wind into fantastic shapes, some of them covered with odd, stunted trees. A current moved up toward the strait, as if trying to push them back into Lake Huron, back into innocence, but they were bound now for Chicago.

Ahab had learned to chart a course with careful precision. He said he had fingers that responded equally well to the work of a compass or fuse. "I'm a delicate guy," he said with a laugh. It seemed that he was always laughing these days, and Liza thought it was because he desired to make them all happy. Perhaps he was gifted with that kind of emotional generosity, although she hadn't noticed it at first. At first, he had seemed dour and restrained, but something had changed. She thought he had changed almost exactly when she had climbed in the empty bunk and waited for him, but she might have been wrong about that. She might have been seeing the change in the way she wanted to see it.

The speed of the lake's current varied. "It's indecisive," Ahab said. "Like a woman I know."

Gil had somehow receded. He took the day watch, sitting near the helm, smoking a mixture of hash and tobacco and discoursing on the problems that awaited workers if they didn't make peace with their black brothers. He'd learned to trim the sails according to the wind and enjoyed pointing out to the others when a sail needed to be hauled in because the wind had moved aft. Ahab's night watch consisted of only himself and Pegasus, and they decided to set fewer sails then and, whenever possible, find a dredged canal or shoal offshore where they could drop anchor and wait for light. Liza had suggested that they shouldn't draw attention to the boat because it was an oddity on this huge, industrial lake.

One night, Ahab argued that they should sail. There were no good spots to anchor, he pointed out, and besides, it was already the end of September. They needed to be in Chicago soon.

"But the wind has shifted south," Liza countered, "and there's no way to stay close to shore without you and Pegasus wearing yourselves out tacking sails hour after hour."

"We'll take a long leg across the lake, then tack south in the morning."

Acquiescing, she made a pot of thick coffee and carried it up on deck. It was the least she could do for the night watch. Pegasus was just then waking, straggling up, pulling on his coat, moving in the chilly air and testing it. Was a hat needed? An extra layer under the coat?

Liza poured a cup of coffee for Gil, who sat in the deckhouse, filling out the log at the end of his watch as she had taught him to do. Joyce was talking to him as he wrote. "But why pick on that poor old statue in Haymarket Square? What possible difference is that going to make?"

Gil moved his pencil over the pages of the log, describing wind and sails and speed as he spoke. "The statue is absolutely significant. We don't hurt a soul and we make an important point."

"It's a statue commemorating a cop," Joyce said sternly.

"I know that. Precisely." Gil pushed his stool back, and Liza noticed that it looked wobbly; a rung had come unstuck. Pegasus slouched through the deckhouse. He cast Liza a long-suffering look.

"Your idea of doing something in Haymarket is to remind people of the labor dispute and the cops who shot the workers there? That was a hundred years ago," Joyce said. "It seems a little abstract. Who's going to remember?"

"Oh, honey, everybody is going to remember. We'll make pamphlets reminding them. We'll blow up the statue, and when the press gets hold of it, they'll finish the picture for everyone. They'll draw all the conclusions we want. That's their job and they just can't help doing it, can they?" He smiled at Joyce. "But it gets better," he said.

Liza asked, "You're planning to blow up a statue?" *Good,* she thought, *no one hurt, but a real message sent.* And the supply of dynamite below would be depleted.

"It'll be prophetic," Gil said. "It'll help the groups coming into town endorse our principles more quickly. It'll give them something to rally around."

"It'll be significant," Rachel chimed in from outside the deckhouse. Then she stuck her head inside. "I mean, historically. Something to define the action after the fact." She looked at Gil. "Don't you think?"

"That's what I said."

Ahab had been trimming his beard below deck. Now he came up, clippers in hand. "I'll have some of that." He indicated the coffee, then smiled at Liza. "Thank you. Ten feet of bronze." He took a sip. "That'll take five or six sticks, one clock, two blasting caps." He forced a laugh, putting both his hands on Liza's shoulders, so she felt herself relax.

"Let's use it all up," Liza said.

"It's in the engine room where it's plenty cool enough."

They had moved the box of dynamite out of the refrigerator because all of them were suffering from headaches. Stored in the cool engine room, behind a steel door, the dynamite seemed to have no effect on them.

"Shouldn't we practice first? Do we know what we're doing?" Pegasus put in. He'd given the helm to Rachel and was crowded in the deckhouse with the others, drinking from Joyce's cup.

Ahab said, "Peg, we're sick of your chicken shit."

"You could've put us in a jam by breaking into that warehouse in broad daylight."

"It was cool," Gil announced with customary finality. "Get off Ahab's back."

Gil and Ahab were fierce allies now that the dynamite was on board. The day Liza, Joyce, and Rachel were arrested in Detroit, Gil had masterminded the theft of the dynamite and blasting caps, though they now knew that Ahab had acted mostly alone, climbing a back fence, braving a guard dog, and then using pure nerve to slip into a warehouse. All this while the five men working there ate lunch, drank coffee, and smoked cigarettes. "The dog was the worst," Gil said afterward, "but Ahab's got a way with animals."

The night made the boat's movement intimate. Except for the light from the deckhouse and the faint glow of the compass near the helm, they were in darkness, rocking forward.

Liza remembered playing at the public pool years ago, when she was a little girl. She had arrived with her mother and immediately launched herself into the water, not coming out for the whole day. Below the water she could see blurred faces, long, bare legs. She'd met another girl and they'd spent the day together in the water, barely coming up for air. Playing tea party. They dove under water then sank to the bottom where they sat cross-legged and pretended to pour tea into cups. The air draining from their lungs in bubbles that rose to the surface, they pushed themselves to stay down longer, pretending to smile and make garbled conversation. The intimacy of being surrounded by water, of impossibly distorted chatter. Underwater you could hold or touch without repercussions. Night sailing was like that.

Like being on a train at three in the morning, blackness in every direction and the silent passengers sharing the intimate gestures of half-lit lives.

It was impossible to see the sails. The lit compass floating in front of the helm was a comfort in the darkness, a signal of direction and meaning. When it was his turn to steer, Ahab sat quietly by himself in front of it, looking up at the sails. "Not looking, listening," he explained, since he could tell by the luffing whether they were full of wind and could adjust course accordingly.

When Gil went below to sleep, Liza stayed on deck. She sat near Ahab and watched him listen. The sight of this man, so new to sailing, so competent, tugged at her. He seemed to live without sentiment. "Aren't you going below?" he asked after a while.

"Can't." And it was true. It made her restless to think of going below where Gil lay.

Ahab laughed. "You're trying to keep us all safe, aren't you?" He bent down and kissed her hair, which was blowing across one side of her face. Now she stood up and put her body behind his at the helm, holding his hands, which held the wooden pegs.

In the morning, orange sunlight seeped over the horizon and slipped across the water till the boat seemed to float on an oily haze. When the day watch was mustered on deck, Gil came up last, going straight to the deckhouse to read the night's events in the log. Ahab was at the bow trimming the headsails. As he dropped a coiled line on the deck, she took his hand. "Come below," she said, tilting her head to one side. "Come on, you've earned it."

She had chosen to become part of the night watch.

A CHILD

They sat in Merril's back yard on patio chairs with the dog between them. "My father calls him Rogue," Mere said, stroking the dog's ears, "He found him in the ravine, running wild."

"Which ravine?" Mark knew she had no idea what the word meant.

Caught, Mere shrugged.

"Anyway," Mark announced, "he wasn't wild. He was somebody's. He acts like he's been having his stomach scratched all his life."

"My father has just as much right to Rogue as anybody, if he found him." For an instant, Mere remembered Mark's first night on board. How she'd taught him to haul up a bucket of water and brush his teeth in it. Then splash the bucket back into the lake, more water, another bucket to wash his face. He was older than she was by four years, but she'd always felt, on the boat, that he needed her teaching. Now their roles were reversed.

Mark said, "Faye would think it was all right. A dog belongs to the air." With that they both laughed.

Then, because he had waited long enough to say it, Mark said, "She needs to talk to you. Tell you something. Important." This was the message Faye had given him to repeat. But he was afraid as soon as he spoke that he'd emphasized the wrong parts of it. "She's not acting normal."

"She's never been normal." The dog rolled over, and Mere moved her fingernails through his fur while Mark put a hand over hers. They sat like that for a few minutes, paying attention to the dog.

Mark tried again. "She needs to talk to you, Mere."

Mere felt a familiar stiffening in her back. "What time is it?"

He sighed.

Three o'clock, she thought. Without her ceremony, without touching the clock, how would she keep them safe? There was a clock above the fireplace in the biggest room. It would have to do. "Come on." She took Mark's hand. "Let's go inside."

"They look sad," Mark said a moment later in the basement. "Stuck in a cage like that." He poked his fingers through the wires, and the birds shifted uneasily.

"He has a shop with birds and fish from all around the world." Mere wasn't going to let Mark's sour opinion change hers. "I'll bet my father's been to a lot of different countries."

Mark let go of the cage. "If Faye didn't tell you about him, there was probably a pretty good reason."

"Why do you always see everything her way? Why

aren't you ever on my side?" Mere threw herself onto a sofa. She had meant to signal to him that she had her own ideas and opinions now that she was away from her mother's boat, but lying here, facedown on the sofa, she was surprised to find that her cheeks were hot. She'd been holding back tears since Mark had appeared at the gate.

He sat beside her. "There's only one side," he said. And at these words Mere began to cry, putting her head on his lap. Mark was quiet, watching a thin streak of sunshine from the high basement window make slow progress through the room. He listened to Mere cry and to the conversation of the birds. When Mere turned to face him, still resting her head in his lap, he wanted to say something. "What about me?" Mark wanted to ask again, since she seemed to feel no responsibility for him. Instead, he reached under her shirt, resting the flat of his palm on her ribs.

"Don't be sad," she said. "I just need to stay here for a while." She had almost convinced herself. Yes. She might even stay. A little longer. "My father needs me. He's never had a chance to get to know me. He wants to know me and I want to know him." Mark didn't say anything, so she went on. "If I don't, one day I'll be grown up and he'll be dead, and we won't ever have talked about a single thing."

"I guess," Mark said.

There was an uncertain waver in his voice that allowed her to ask, "Don't you ever miss your parents?" She moved her own hand under her shirt and placed it flat on top of his. It was a question she'd asked many times before in many guises, but he'd never been willing to answer. Sitting with his hand over her beating heart and her hand over his, he wanted more than ever to tell her. To come clean. *Telling her will attach her to me.* Then he thought about his promise to Faye, a promise he'd made years before. Faye said that Mere must not hear the story because Mere must not think that badness went unpunished. If Mark told Mere the story, he would be able to lie to Faye. No problem. This ability to lie was inside him. But it was not inside Mere. Mere hadn't been trained in deception. She would never be able to hide anything from her mother. He didn't answer.

After a moment, Mere pushed his hand away. "Sorry I asked."

✦

Faye waited. She found it stranger than anything to be alone. The water was still, the boat, intractable, nudged up in the marsh and mud. *If we don't move soon, we'll freeze over*, she thought, remembering that fairy tale of the boy who has to free his sister from the ice palace and thaw her heart.

Mere's clock deep in the mud of the lagoon. Hands frozen. Time stopped.

Cattails bristled, their thick brown ends like sticks of dynamite. Snow swirled, disappearing on the wind. There was no sun in the sky, only an absence of darkness. Mark would come back with Mere.

She could not leave the ship—how would Mere find her? She could not leave the city—how would Mere find her? They might be coming—American FBI in Canada—but she had to wait. What she needed was to keep busy. Not stand on the deck in plain view or pace by the lighthouse smoking cigarettes. *Resort to action*, Faye told herself, descending below deck and dragging the pump out from under the sink in the galley.

She opened the heavy hatch to the engine room.

While she waited for the children, Faye lifted the deck boards and pumped out the water and diesel that filled the bilge. The task gave her a guilty pleasure because it involved emptying their polluted, oily water into the lake. One truth about living on a boat was that it slowly contributed to the contamination of its most vital element. But as Faye saw it, this was a truth about living anywhere. The point was to minimize damage. She had learned this lesson the hard way.

Chicago. Gil was the first back to the *Persephone*, grabbing a dangling rope and pulling himself aboard, then lifting off the motorcycle helmet and wiping the black grease from his face with a sleeve. He hurried to the deckhouse, threw the gears into neutral, and started the engine. As she rushed to the boat through a maze of industrial warehouses, Liza could hear the engine bell sound. Gil was already loosing the lines when she struggled down the dock with Ahab, who was bleeding and crying, a shirt swollen with blood pressed against his shoulder. "He needs a doctor," she called out to Gil.

Ahab growled at her. "No way! They'll lock me up. I'm not going."

Gil had the bowline in his hand. "Fuck it, Liza. Whoever's not here in the next five minutes gets left behind."

Again Ahab was adamant, "No, we don't leave them here."

Liza could not seem to control her hands. They began to tremble now. Her teeth were chattering. Images jumped in and out of her head. The smashed glass of the bank. The rioters jumping up and down. A gun. A raised steel rod. A terrible dark face. The face of a policeman. What had she done? *He's alive,* she told herself. *I'm not strong enough to kill.* Where were the others? And Ahab, bleeding, in her arms. Something terrible. Terribly wrong.

Now Rachel and Joyce were on the dock. "We're staying here."

"What do you mean?" A voice from the deck.

Rachel was out of breath, her chest heaving, the black grease smeared over her pale skin. "It's more risky if we all go."

Had they seen? Liza whispered, "What happened?"

"He's passed out," Joyce said, studying Ahab and sounding surprised, as if she'd noticed for the first time that something was wrong.

Gil said, "We need your help, for Chrissake. Look at Liza. She's out of it! Help me get him on deck." But it was Pegasus who dragged Ahab aboard. He arrived at that moment, feet pounding down the length of the dock. Pegasus with another boy, someone they didn't know. "Who is that?"

"He's coming. He was detained. They'll reclassify

him." With the help of the stranger, Pegasus pulled Ahab onto the boat.

Rachel and Joyce released the last lines and watched them set off.

They left under cover of night, sails doused, pulling into the stream of freighter traffic, a bedraggled vessel swept away by a flood. There was a new passenger. Yes, it was fine, Liza told herself. What difference could it make? She made herself look in the eyes of this new boy, Earl, who was also afraid. She told herself that he needed her protection, although what she wanted was to run to her cabin and close the door for good.

The next morning, Gil was sullen, unnaturally quiet. Ahab, nervous and cross, nursed his bandaged shoulder. Pegasus, uncharacteristically, kept himself below deck and apart. Over the radio, they heard the report. Twenty protesters injured, the windows of a bank blown out. Estimated damage to property in the neighborhood of Lincoln Park was said to be in the hundreds of thousands. They heard what Liza most feared to hear: a policeman was dead.

Her only friends looked horrified.

They would not rest for three days, until they had put a good distance between themselves and that report. Gil managed to connect, by radio telephone, with Carl at his bookstore. They needed identity papers and Carl had experience. Did they trust Carl? Did they trust anyone now? They had not put enough food on board to last them the weeks it would take to reach Toledo, but they would find supplies once they were out of Lake Michigan, where they imagined they would somehow be less noticeable.

Meanwhile, Liza did not eat and refused to cook, complaining of nausea, dizziness. She sat at the bow, keeping a firm eye on the horizon, sometimes vomiting, sometimes lying quietly with her head on Earl's lap. She did not know him, and that fact was comforting, if anything was. For hours, she studied the mole on his left cheek, the slight indentation at his hairline, the bone of his wrist. For hours, they said nothing to each other, since talking made her feel queasy and Earl preferred silence to anything else.

Pegasus sometimes talked to Earl, telling him how to stay out of the way and how to be useful when usefulness was an asset. Now it was always Gil or Ahab at the helm—one or the other—and they set all sails, to keep up their speed. The wind was a muscle, something to push them clear of the action that had gone so wrong. The wind could right the past, carrying them out of Lake Michigan while the last leaves clung to October branches, while they rode through a human storm.

Farther north, the branches were bare and the wind was colder, and they slept in one cabin to conserve heat. They slept as one body, although for Ahab and Gil, the alliance was now uneasy, forged in the face of adversity. "We'll stay in Canadian waters," Ahab told the others, pointing to the chart and moving a finger along the northern shore of Lake Huron, a lake Earl had never seen.

On the eighteenth day out, they dropped Earl in Goderich, Ontario, where a sleepy dock master told Gil that there were certain "points" required of visitors to Canada who desired to immigrate. "You bring money?" he asked Earl. "You gotta wife or a job waiting up here? I could let you in as a visitor but you got no guarantee. You can't stay on indefinitely."

Liza would gladly have married Earl to keep him safe, but instead she gave him her last fifty dollars. During their voyage across Lake Michigan, she had begun to believe that carrying this innocent—this draft dodger—away from the Vietnam war might be a way to propitiate her crime.

She could not smile at Earl when he left. The lake was too full of bile, the sky too busy, and her hands still trembling. She hardly raised her head, imprisoned in a fog of fear and uneasiness, especially when the boat docked. It was the sight of land, she decided, that now made her sick.

Could anything else make her feel so tender, so sore inside, so weak? Could regret cause her to go down to her cabin to weep? "It's because I can't keep anything down," she told Gil, to excuse herself. "It's the dynamite."

Ahab, grimacing in pain, hoisted the box of dynamite up out of the engine room. "It's evidence now, anyway." He used a crowbar to ease off the lid, then tossed the sticks one by one out into the lake. For a long time, they floated, appearing to follow the boat in a line of exclamation and causing gulls to flap down for a closer look. When at last they disappeared from sight, Ahab lashed a metal chain to the box and threw it over, watching it sink, while Liza stared at the horizon and thought of her father's wrench, her father's ashes.

The feeling of sickness did not abate. Now, at last, she considered another possibility. How long had it been since she had bled?

Fugitives, she thought. Impossible to create a child in

these circumstances. Out of what? The idea of pregnancy was too unreal to be real, but looked at another way, they had traveled to Chicago and someone there—a policeman—was now dead. She had been part of a life-and-death struggle. Here was another piece of it.

"When we get to Carl's, he'll set you up with a doctor. Easy to fix," Gil told her.

"What do you want to do?" Ahab asked.

"I don't know. I can't think." What she wanted was to sail into Toledo as it had been a few months ago, in sunlight, the sails bright. In innocence.

"There's no choice here," Gil said flatly. "You're going underground. Christ, you could be picked up any minute, Liza, and you wouldn't put a baby through that would you?"

It occurred to her that Gil was claiming the baby, if such a baby existed. He was announcing ownership and destroying it at the same time. But was it Gil's child? When had they last been together? Already she was beginning the fugitive's life, not remembering dates and times, only cities, identities.

She turned her back on Gil and faced Ahab, putting her two hands in his. "I can't go to a doctor."

Gil said, "Sure you can, Liza. We'll get one we can trust."

Ahab said, "I don't think that's what she means."

Though she would have the child, though she and Ahab now slept together in her father's cabin, Gil did not leave them in Toledo as Liza had expected he would.

Instead, Pegasus went to the bookstore and returned

with more than new birth certificates. He also brought a friend of Carl's—another dodger hoping to ride the boat across the water to Canada. "This is Tony," Pegasus said, passing the envelope of papers up to Gil. Tony tossed his bag on deck as Pegasus announced, "I'm taking off."

Liza opened the envelope Gil handed her and began to understand her new life. There were two small identity cards, one for Merril Holmes and one for his wife. "So I'm Faye Holmes now," she said dully, "a person too dangerous to know. Is that it, Peg? Is that why you're leaving us?"

Pegasus told her that he'd had enough of life on the cramped and chilly boat. It had nothing to do with risk.

When they pulled away from Toledo, it was Ahab—now Merril Holmes—who stood by her side. But Gil stayed with them. They were a strained and uncomfortable trio. She did not ask Gil why he had remained because it would be almost impossible, now, to sail the boat without him.

In a sliver of mirror above the sink, she squinted, remembering herself. A pair of scissors heavy in her hand, held just above her scalp, she sliced her hair off in clumps, watching it fall into the metal basin. The police had photographed the riot—she was certain of it. This meant they had a picture of her face. Would the haircut be enough? She focused on the mirror. Nineteen years old, with dark rings under her eyes, bruised cheeks.

She would burn the ship's registration papers, burn them in this sink... but when she slid back the drawer of the chart table, she saw the box with her father's ashes.

Did she have a right to carry him anymore? He would not approve of a fugitive ship or a fugitive daughter. To make him take this journey with her, leaving behind name and nation, would be a betrayal. But when she poured the ashes of paper and burned hair into the churning gray wake, she could not bring herself to do the same with her father. *Leave him be. Let him wait with the compass and the pencils, beside the charts and under the log. Or should that go too?* Yes. The log was a record of the *Persephone*'s past. She pulled it off the sloping table and carried it to the metal sink, enjoying the feel of its smooth cover and the familiar *click* of its soft pages under her fingers.

At the sink, she began, two or three at a time, to rip the pages out.

But she could not allow herself to destroy them. Like her father's ashes, they were all that connected her to her own life. Although she was ashamed of this sentiment, she hid the pages behind the stovepipe.

As winter passed and spring came on, they took two more boys across to Canada. Faye Holmes was visibly pregnant, carrying her child narrow and high. She'd decided it must be a boy.

"I'm not ready for a son," Merril said. "Light your candles for a girl. Boys are too much worry."

Gil snorted. He was the only one of them on the boat who didn't need false papers to keep him safe. Why did he stay? Faye lay on the bunk wondering this, sleeping fitfully and dreaming, always dreaming of the face, then Ahab bloody, and Gil starting the engine, pointing the bow away from Chicago. Why did Gil stay? Because being with two fugitives was as good a rebellion as any, maybe, or because he could not imagine leaving Ahab—Merril—the steeler who had once saved his skin. Or, maybe, just maybe, because he was in some way responsible since he'd led them into that October storm.

On a windless day in July when the pains began, Faye asked Merril to come with her down into the forepeak because she wanted to be inside its tight, narrow space, holding onto the ladder that gave her a way to resist. "It hurts so much," she told him. "I won't be able to stand it. I don't want Gil to hear me scream."

Merril built her a nest of old shirts and towels, any clean cloth he could find on top of the bins of anchor chains and rope and told her to breathe quickly and count, to breathe and then pant. Without wind, the sails sagged. The swells seemed to come from nowhere. Faye heard the widow-maker knocking on the deck above. She leaned into Merril and pleaded with him to stop the noise. He pushed her hair off her forehead and told her to pant.

This must have gone on for hours, her leaning into him, holding the ladder, and Merril telling her not to push. It did not occur to her to wonder how he knew about this business of birth. During the time in the forepeak and for many weeks after, she simply trusted him.

The widow-maker stopped and the sails filled. They could hear the lake slosh against the hull and Faye understood that the boat was following wind. When the baby crowned, it was Merril who yelled.

Faye named the child Mere for the lake where she'd been born, for the man who'd held her through it all, and because she had decided the baby was his, although she had no real evidence. Faye clutched at the newborn's skin, sniffed at it, and pushed her face against the scalp. As if she had been pulled from the lake itself, Mere's eyes were sealed shut, but her tiny mouth opened in a great yelp as she took her first earthly breath.

Then Faye and Merril lay listening to Mere take up her beat and howl—along with the wind, the war, and the winter ahead.

For three years, the *Persephone* crisscrossed the lake, carrying draft dodgers out of the United States and into safety. Some of the boys had already had their numbers drawn and had to cross into Canadian waters hidden under the *Persephone*'s bunks. Once in Canada, they emerged, relieved of one fear and facing another: they would have to make a new life. They could never go home. Eventually Merril found a sympathetic immigration officer who would close his eyes, ignore the points, and stamp the paperwork.

At any given time, one or two of these boys might be on the boat. Chickens hopped around the decks and produced the occasional egg. Tomato plants grew in cans placed where they would not get tangled in the lines. They bought most of the food on shore with money they earned panhandling in the ports. Faye stayed far away from this activity. Most of the time they sailed, and that kept down the cost of diesel for the engine. They did what they could to avoid attention, following the "seaman's rules of the road." Although Gil argued that even these modest regulations were concocted by a police state, they were not in a position to question anyone's rules.

Their lake was the smallest of those great lakes carved out by the glaciers as they receded at the end of the last ice age. Bounded on the south by the state of New York and on the north by the province of Ontario, where farmland rises gently from the shore and spreads out in broad plains, vineyards, and forests. In the winter of 1973, Merril suggested that the three of them, with the child, put the *Persephone* in dry dock for an overhaul and find a place to live, quietly, on the Canadian side. "We've dropped enough boys off, we know how to disappear," he said. "And a winter on the boat with Mere is going to be murder." He gauged their reactions by their expressions: Gil's was somber, interested, possibly tempted, but Faye's was stubborn, fixed against the idea. "Is it Canada you don't want?" Merril challenged her. "Or is it any piece of land?"

It was raining that afternoon with a cold wind blowing in from the southwest. Gil had noted all of this in the day's log along with surface current and location at noon. He had added, in parentheses, "seasonal variation of mood" because they had had this argument the previous winter.

Faye went into their cabin and pulled Mere out of the bunk. The child woke fiercely, as if being torn from the lull of the boat, its creaking and groaning, its perfectly understood rocking. She stopped crying when Faye brought her into the warm deckhouse where Gil and Merril sat, but she rubbed her eyes and shoveled into her mother's shoulder and hair, refusing to look around or smile.

Gil leaned back on the broken stool and watched. In Faye's arms, Mere was listening and still. Faye stroked her hair with one hand, balancing the frame of the child on one arm, while Mere clung to her mother's waist with tight legs. She refused to be put down when Faye tried to sit her on the chart table. Instead she grabbed harder at her mother and began to fuss.

Merril turned away as if he could no longer bear to watch them. The *Persephone* was riding the swells off Hamilton harbor. Beyond it, pear and apple trees had been picked over and left to rest, vines had been cleaned, and the fields lay empty and wet. "I, for one, am getting off," he announced quickly. "Whatever you two decide."

"Three," Faye put in quietly. "Don't you think Mere has a vote in this?"

"No, I do not." With that, he forced his way past her and out.

"Watch her for me," Faye whispered, shoving Mere so quickly at Gil that neither could protest, and rushing out of the deckhouse.

She found Merril in the galley splicing new lines that would be heavy enough and strong enough to hold the boat to the dock during winter storms. He was good at it, spreading the braided lines apart and weaving the tail ends back on themselves. She sat down, watching him work, clouds of breath, like steam from an engine, coming out of his mouth. They were silent for a long time, then she put her hands on his shoulders, but he shrugged them off.

She said, "What if we find a dock somewhere, maybe one of the islands in the St. Lawrence, some place rural? We can sleep on the boat, cook on the boat, but set up a camp on land."

Still he was silent. His breath.

"It's a compromise." She looked at the line thickening in his hand, and realized that he'd already decided to stay with them. Why splice ropes to be used in winter if he expected the boat to be hauled out? Though he'd agreed, his silence was meant to punish her for binding him. *It takes thick ropes to hold your ship in winter*, she reminded herself. And left him working there.

Slowly winter passed, and when the long days of sunlight returned at last, contentment seemed to come too. Faye spent her hours near the helm, quilting, something her mother had taught her to do, with both eyes closed if necessary. Moment by moment, she concentrated, not on the toddler who was beside her or on the boat and its fluttering, lapping sails, but on the tiny stitches—even, even—that came from her careful fingers. Her mother had sewn acres of quilts as a testament to hours spent alone, hours her husband spent at the plant and then on the boat, away from her. When Faye's father was about to arrive, she would jab her needle into a patch of cloth, fold up the whole bundle, and tuck it into a satchel. Then she'd say to her child, "Never let a man see you work." But Faye didn't think of the quilts as work, although they provided a form of income. She made them from ensigns they liberated from harbors and yacht clubs. *A flag belongs to the air.* And she cut the quilt pieces small enough so that no one could tell where the fabric came from. They had silkiness. Bright colors, strange crests. The symbols seemed somehow familiar, but Faye lived in a world where every color meant exactly nothing. Even, even. In, out. Green, blue, lovely blue. These days she rarely spoke to the men and was easy only when there was no shore, no landmark to be seen.

Merril cut the engine, and began the slow work of setting sails.

Gil was below taking a nap, and when Faye suggested waking him, Merril chided, "Let him rest." There wasn't much wind, so he lashed a line around the helm and set off down the deck, unbagging sails as he went.

Slowly the sun emerged from behind the morning cloud.

Slowly the quilt grew in Faye's hands.

Mere played in the trough hollowed out of the deck around the helm. She sat in a pile of scraps, decorating her body, tossing bits of cloth like feathers into the air. As the sails rose up, so did the wind, and Faye gathered the scraps into the bag at her feet, telling Mere that otherwise they would leave a trail in the water like crumbs to mark the way.

When he'd set the mainsail and the jib, Merril climbed the rigging, ratline by ratline, and called down to Faye, "Whoa. Look at me, Holmes!" He liked to use her name because it was also his.

"Looking good, Holmes!" She could not look at him without putting a hand over her eyes. He was too much to take in all at one time.

Merril swung himself carefully onto the spreader at the top of the mast and looked down.

Mere was staring at herself in the brass binnacle when suddenly the wind rose, catching the massive mainsail from behind and sending the whole weight of it swinging across the deck.

The boom cracked and the ship pitched to one side.

Faye snapped around in time to see Mere roll under the rail and into the lake. She stood then, the quilt flying from her lap like a bandage to mark the wound in the water. She heard the sky open, a flutter like the penitent sails, and saw Merril dive through the air, a muscle tensed, an arrow whose target was the glare of the floating quilt.

He entered the water and disappeared into the underworld.

Without breathing, Faye let the light on the water remind her of something. What she would be without Mere. Peeled open.

Then Merril pierced the surface again, clutching Mere's tiny waist with his hands. He treaded water, lowering Mere onto one shoulder and pounding her back, lake water streamed from her nose and mouth.

Faye's legs began to move. She found her hands untying the line from the helm. She turned the boat into the wind, tacking the mainsail, waiting for the boat to gain momentum, then tacking again and bringing it down. She moved along the deck to the gangway and reached between the rails for her child.

Mere coughed up water.

"I have you." Faye lifted Mere, and held on. The words *man overboard* came to her then, too late.

The night Mere drowned and came back, Faye spread her bunk with a quilt and put the child to sleep on it. The quilt was blue and green to make sense of the terrible thing that had happened. Faye feared that her child would never feel safe again, and she watched Mere's eyelids close—another drowning. What horrified Faye was not Mere moving backward, leaving the boat, but the boat moving forward, leaving Mere, while she, Faye, stood on deck watching.

Gil came into the cabin. "She all right?" Faye nodded. "I'll watch her a little while," he offered.

Stooping so that she wouldn't hit the bulkhead, Faye stood up, backed out of her cabin, and climbed the ladder into the deckhouse, then moved out onto the deck. Anchored, the boat rode beneath stars that hung like beacons. The night wind had risen, and the boat pointed into it, like a hound. Faye's feet felt the smooth worn wood as she padded toward the foredeck where Merril was sitting.

"She's holding," he said, and it was a second before Faye realized that he meant the anchor line. She leaned into him.

"How's she doing?" he asked.

"Holding." A gust of wind blew the anchor light above, and their shadows wavered. They sat like that for a long time, the boat shifting with the wind, the anchor light swinging on the end of its line.

The next day, when Mere complained that her ear hurt, the three adults dripped warm vegetable oil into it, sang songs, and read to her. But as hours ticked by and the three-year-old twisted and cried in pain, Merril said he was making for land, where they would search out a doctor. The engine rang to life, and he turned to Gil. "Douse the sails."

"Are you crazy?" Faye shouted at Merril. She handed the child to Gil and strode across the deck. "We're on the American side here and I'm not going to jail because of an earache. Mere will be fine any minute now, won't you, baby?"

"We're putting to shore, and if you don't like it, you can swim or sink." He shoved her away from the helm, keeping the wooden pegs tight in his hand. With the *Persephone*'s sails still flying, he swung the bow towards the wind, so that the wind backed the sails and stalled them. "Jesus, Gil, douse them."

"No," Faye said, shaking her head vehemently. "No, no, no. How does it help Mere to lose us?" She reached out, but Merril brushed her off.

"Better to go deaf and spend the rest of her life reading lips trying to find out what the hell happened to her out here!" he shouted. "You're a selfish monster, Liza! Wasn't her nearly drowning enough of a sign for you that we can't live this way."

A violent shriek overhead, and then the flap and howl of the square sail as it ripped. Merril spun the helm away from the wind, and the boat dipped precariously, causing him to lose his footing.

Faye took advantage of the moment, grabbing the helm and shoving Merril so he fell to his knees. "Forget your plan. I'm in charge." She was glaring, frantic, teeth almost bared as he got to his feet again. "It's *your* selfishness we're dealing with. Always. Always. You want to leave, and you use a baby's pain as your means of escape." She yanked at the helm so fiercely that the *Persephone* dipped to windward and the mainsail swung hard across the stern. Gil and the child fell against the deckhouse, while Merril had to duck to avoid the boom. "Hard a lee!" Faye shouted wildly.

"You can't be trusted to take care of yourself anymore, let alone a kid! You pick at your quilts and stare at your hands feeling sorry for yourself but what good does that do? What happened in Chicago is in the past now! It's over—"

"You want to leave," Faye interrupted. "That's all this is. An excuse. You're sick of the boat and you don't care what happens to us."

Merril moved off to the deckhouse, suddenly silent. She could see him now for what he was. A man like her father who was capable, who knew how to splice a rope or make an engine run. It was this ability, this physicality and energy that had allowed her to feel safe with him. But with that energy came the threat that he might at any time explode. A house ablaze.

She saw now how impossible it must have been for her mother, trying to rein in a man who wanted no horizon, and now here she was trying to hold on to a man who was too unstable to be confined. She remembered his first night aboard. He'd paced the ship as if memorizing its dimensions—the step down from the aft deck to the foredeck, the broken plank near the anchor chain. He'd been learning the possibilities of this world, and also the restrictions.

When Merril shoved his clothes and papers into an oily canvas bag, Faye went up on deck and refused to watch. *He'll be back*, she thought, but it was Gil who pleaded with him, "What're we going to do on this boat without you?"

"I'm the muscle, the steeler, but I don't get a say in how my kid is raised. Is that it?"

"Don't be an asshole." Gil was angry. "You leave and you won't be able to raise this kid at all."

Now Merril stopped packing his bag. He turned and looked at Gil squarely. "What're you doing here, anyway? You're not at risk, you aren't wanted. What the fuck are you doing here?"

"The boat. I thought you needed my help."

Merril's gray eyes were level, beaded. "That's bullshit, you never could stand that she was my kid. Now you've got her all to yourself, so enjoy." He threw the bag over his shoulder and moved to the ladder. "See how it feels to get what you want."

He reached above the stove and found the gun wrapped in its cloth, and put it in his bag. Then he barged into Faye's cabin without knocking, took the baby from her arms before she could resist him, and said something only Mere could hear. Turning his back on Faye, he put the child down and drew his shoulders up, as if he expected to be shot from behind; then he pushed himself out of the cabin.

A MEETING

The neighborhood around Cabbagetown was at its best in autumn, Merril thought. Its small, cramped cottages—built for German laborers—had come up a peg or two. Old floors refinished, stained glass in the windows, young couples moving in and repainting the trim. The outsides looked good now, especially with the trees all yellowish and orange and the yards full of wet leaves. Old neighborhoods come out of the bad times. *Like me*, he thought, *a steeler made good.*

The neighborhood was tight, confining, but full of atmosphere of a kind. He navigated the narrow streets, one hand on the wheel, the other on Ellie's thigh, a weighted presence meant to comfort. After all, he had given her a scare. Shit, he should've remembered to get rid of the note, she wouldn't have been any the wiser. Still she was taking it in stride, had cooked the girl crepes, made conversation. That was a beginning. The next step was his.

"You can just drop me here," Ellie was saying, pointing

to the church. Merril pulled over and reached across her to open her door, as if he did not want her to stall.

Grabbing her bag, she leaned over to kiss Merril on the neck. "I'll be done in an hour, hour and a half. Can you pick me up?"

"Sure."

"Be good."

"Last thing on my mind." When he put a hand on her arm, he felt her muscles twitch. "You do it for me every time," he said, pulling back and glancing at the building's dark entrance.

Ellie got out and he inhaled, as if holding himself in check. She wore a black leotard and tights, with thick woolen warmers around her ankles. Merril watched her walk up the sidewalk and into her dance class. What happened in there was a mystery as far as he was concerned. Another mystery was what to say when he got to Gil's office.

It ought to be easy enough. Merril swung the car around a corner and down Parliament Street. The snow was thickening, and the car slid on the streetcar tracks. He turned another corner, drove for a while, checking the rearview and looking at the numbers on buildings. He'd never been to Gil's office; in fact, he and Gil hadn't really kept in touch. They'd have to talk about that.

It was a narrow building exposed on two sides. *Shit*, he thought, *is there a side entrance?* He drove on, rolling down his window, leaning out. Did Gil live downtown or had he bought out in the suburbs? He'd be married. Kids?

As it hit the windows, the snow melted. He turned on his wipers and they dragged across the glass. He circled the block. Where would he park? Not outside the office. He'd park it in the lot on King, then use a back stairwell. He turned another corner. And how to start the conversation? "Ancient history," he said aloud, trying out the sound in his mouth, enjoying the words that seemed to exonerate him.

"Ancient history," he said to Gil a few minutes later. "I can't even remember being that screwed up. But we were. It was different back then." He looked around at the bland office, the city outside with its civilizing indifference, the two of them standing there in clean shirts. "Fuck," he said with a genial laugh, "what a couple of idealists we were," and he said this with a decidedly Canadian ring, as if he'd outgrown all that was unrealistic and childish along with his accent when he came across the lake. He wondered whether he sounded defensive.

"It's been a long time." Gil pointed to a decanter on his file cabinet without inviting Merril to help himself to it. He gestured toward an overstuffed chair piled with papers, as if he had never had visitors before and said, "Why don't we establish a sitting place," which Merril assumed was a means of keeping the meeting businesslike. Gil swept the papers off the chair and moved around to his own side of the desk.

Merril found himself looking at some of the papers and he felt the other man's eyes on him. "I'm in a bit of a sitcheeation," he said, with the affected pronunciation they had once used as a comradely code.

Gil didn't smile.

"We've known each other since day one, Gil. Literally. You know how it was. We grabbed at anything back then." Merril noticed that Gil leaned back in his chair, putting even more distance between them. "Which is why I took responsibility for you and vice versa. You, me—we were closer than the rest." He couldn't seem to shut up.

Gil nodded a head that was prematurely balding. The bald spot seemed to give him an air of confidence that Merril envied. "Situation?" Gil reached for a glass, wiping it out with his hand, suddenly efficient, as if he wanted to remove himself from Merril's run-on sentences.

"I can't speak for you, but I would say I have no regrets. I got through it and came out the other end." He laughed. "But as it turns out, all these years later, the feds have longer memories than we do. They've finally caught up. They're sitting on my front door."

"Then why would you come here?" Gil asked quickly.

"You're an attorney, right?"

"I'm also a witness to what happened." Gil held the glass in his hand. "Why would you lead them here?"

Merril understood then that Gil was only humiliating him, as he, Merril—on past occasions, many years before, when it suited him—had humiliated Gil. It was true that after the events in Chicago, they'd formed an alliance, but it had always been a struggle. "You misunderstand," he said curtly. "They've caught up, that's all, and I thought that you'd want to know—"

"So let's go through the facts," Gil cut in. "I want you to give me the details exactly."

"Yeah." Merril thought his voice sounded childish. "Right," he said, pushing his shoulders back.

"Why are they letting you know they're watching you? What do they want if it isn't you?"

Merril had known this question was coming. "A conspiracy rap is pretty minor in the scheme of things. I should have known that, but the war, as you know, was breathing down my neck. I should have gone home and cleared things up. It wasn't as bad for me as it was for Faye." He brushed something from his pants.

"You sure this goes that far back?" Gil paused for a minute, tilting his head to the side and considering Merril. True, they had known each other for a long time, but Gil was fairly certain that it had also been a long time since they had liked each other. *You keep your friends close,* he thought. *You keep your enemies closer.*

Merril closed his eyes and shook his head. "I'm asking something simple of my oldest friend." His tone turned it into a question. "Could you talk to Faye, convince her to take me on the boat? It's for her own good."

Now Gil closed his eyes. Then he opened them again. "You think they're after her. Are you saying they'll get her if she doesn't take you back?" He waited a moment, then continued. "As bad as it got in the past, we were never willing to turn our friends in."

Merril struck his forehead dramatically with the palm of his hand. "Jesus, Gil, do you make me out for an asshole. I wouldn't give up Faye. She's the mother of my kid, who happens to be at my house, as I said on the phone."

Gil looked at Merril, trying to read something in his face, but it was a mask of contrition.

"I'm trying to take responsibility for my life," Merril continued. "They need me back on the boat."

Gil looked at both hands. Suddenly he seemed to remember the decanter and lifted it off the file cabinet.

"This stuff's the best," he said, pouring, as if they were again conspirators.

"I told Faye about them. I warned her," Merril said, swallowing his scotch quickly, then glaring down at the empty glass.

Gil turned his glass in his hands, and spoke slowly. "They can't make you testify against Faye. She's your wife."

Merril rocked forward, then back. Forward again, man to man. "She's not my wife, you know that. Never was. If they put me on the stand, I'd have to say that."

"She carries your name!" Gil raised his voice for the first time. "You represented her that way. And gladly. In the eyes of the law, she's your wife," Gil said. He seemed to take perverse pleasure in saying this.

Merril was fumbling now, searching for another appeal. "Old Liza's tough as nails, Gil, don't forget that. Look how she's survived all these years."

Gil winced.

Merril noticed it, but kept going. "I mean, she's got a vein of coldness in her. You never knew her the way I did." He knew this wasn't true, remembered himself looking at the stern of the ship where Faye and Gil and the child stood. The walls of the lock rose beside them, the water churned, and he was left out. Merril let out a sigh. "I knew she'd tangle me up."

"She saved your sorry life." Gil was angry.

"Which is why I have no intention of turning on her. What do you take me for?"

"I take you for what you've been your whole life. I know you whether I want to or not." Gil paused for a moment, letting this comment sink in. "You can't go back to the boat. You've got to see that. It's a risk to her." Another pause. "Who will you give to the FBI?"

"I don't know." Merril sounded defeated. "I'm not a rat." He shifted and wondered whether Gil had bought a big chair to make people feel small. It occurred to him that he'd been wrong to come. Gil had always used his brain like a snare, wrapping it around any piece of illogic. Merril was sweating, his mouth dry. He lifted the empty glass to his lips, put it down again, then said too quickly, "Of course you were there. At the time. You sort of ran the whole show. Planned the statue. The whole damned thing. As I recall it."

Gil had not moved his eyes. He stared at Merril. The stare seemed to take a long time, during which Merril shifted, scratched an ankle, rattled the empty glass. He saw that Gil understood the threat, and continued. "I came to you because you know how to talk. You more than any of us. If you won't talk to Liza, what about talking to the feds?"

Gil studied him for a while longer, then said, "No way, man," coldly affecting the slang they had used with each other in the past. "If you've got trouble with the FBI, it's your trouble. As of today." But what he said scared even himself.

Once Merril had retreated from the room, his glass empty on the table, Gil leaned back in his chair. The feds would be outside the building, so he couldn't go to the harbor.

He thought about this carefully.

Biting his lip, he picked up the phone, and dialed the number he had used off and on over the years to find out whether the *Persephone* was in port. When the dock master answered, Gil asked the question once more.

"Her boat left yesterday, sir. I gave her boy the envelope."

THE RUNAWAY

Faye lay on her back in the *Persephone*'s engine room, watching the bilge drain. The space was cramped, and the steel hull seemed to take all her heat. On the other side of it, inches away, was the water. In wintertime, she often woke to the feeling that the lake and sky together conspired to steal all the heat from the stove, the boat, their bodies. They were alive only to heat the lake and sky.

Faye brought herself back to the present, to the bilge and the smell of diesel, to the engine above her like an animal. When Mark returned to the boat, he would be leading Mere by the hand. Yes. He would arrive with a sullen shadow thrown by the lights that lit the path to Lighthouse Cove like dozens of bright arms. Mere would be angry; she might be furious that Mark had intervened in her plan, but Faye would watch them come toward her through the dark and know that it was Mark, dear Mark, who had brought Mere back to life. Another woman might throw herself into the shaft that lit his shoulders and Mere's braided hair. "Tell me, tell me, please," she might say to the child, "why did you leave me?" Faye was not that woman. She lay in the bilge, silent, waiting for Mark to bring her daughter back. He'd gone down into cold water to retrieve the anchor. He'd made three attempts, but he had done it, had found the eye and lashed the rope to it, had held them all together when wind and wave threatened to tear them apart.

The wind is a muscle, she thought. *If he doesn't return her to me, what will I do? How much longer do I wait?* Could she do what she had never done in all these years? Leave the boat. Go into the city. Find Mere. She must talk to Mere. There was no one left who mattered anymore. She would go to Merril's house. It was risky, she knew, but she would have to do it.

Wait until dark. Darkness would be a hand pushing her, giving her the momentum to cross the harbor into the city.

How much longer till dark? November was stingy. It would get dark early.

Three years before, she'd sailed close enough to Erie to anchor and send Mark across in the rowboat. It had suddenly become necessary to see her mother's house. But she depended on Mark to tell her about it. She did not dare to go there herself. He looked in the windows. But what he described to her was not a family she knew, and she had understood then that her mother was dead. She had found herself worrying, hoping that her mother had died in the summer. If she'd died in winter, how would they have got her into the frozen ground?

Thinking of how she depended on Mark made her remember something else. An afternoon in Belleville, many years before, when Mere was on deck while Faye put a new coat of varnish on the benches around the helm. Mere had received a postcard from one of the boys, and at the end of the postcard he'd written, "P.S. I miss you!" When Faye had explained what *P.S.* meant, the letters had seemed to Mere like a private code. P.S. P.S. P.S. She began to attach them to everything.

"P.S. I'm going below to play," Mere had said.

That day itself had a strange postscript. A group of men sat on the dock, fishing poles dangling in the lake, listening to the news on a portable radio. Dodging between them, his head down, hands shielding his face, a wild-looking boy made straight for the boat as if Faye were expecting him. He jumped off the edge of the dock, over the line that stretched across the gangway, and into her arms. "Hide me!" he said. *Nine or ten years old*, Faye thought, *but made of good mud*. She led him down through the hatch and into the main cabin where the chickens were underfoot. "Mere," she called, her eyes adjusting to the lack of light as she slid a mattress off one of the bunks and lifted the wooden board, gesturing at a small, dark space. *It's musty*, she thought. *It's been years since a boy has hidden in here*. She slid the mattress back on the bunk, and told Mere to take off her clothes and get on top. No one would move a naked child.

Mere did as she was told, and they felt the boat list toward the dock as someone stepped on board. They heard heavy footsteps overhead as Faye moved through the galley toward her cabin, then up onto the deck. "Hello?"

Two of the men were dressed in the same khaki shorts and blue shirt that the boy had been wearing; the other one was in the black uniform of a priest. "We're looking for a runaway," this one said. He was paunchy and wheezing, out of breath. "And we saw him heading off this way."

"There was a boy on the dock earlier," she managed.

By now the fishermen were watching closely, trying to judge what kind of woman she was, Faye imagined. Maybe some of the men were old dodgers. So many of them were out of work, and maybe one of them knew her. Or about her—the Ferry Queen, she'd been called. It dawned on her that this might be the reason they were so quiet.

The priest peered down the main hatch. "Mind if we look?" But before Faye could answer, he had started down. The other two followed.

Faye did not go with them. She feigned indifference, making her way back to the deckhouse. They finally emerged, adjusting their caps, even stamping their feet, and before they stepped off the boat, one of them said, "If you catch sight of him, lady, give us a call up," and handed Faye a worn-out card, wet with his thumbprint. *Father Rolf, Delinquent Services.* As if he understood that she was lying to him, he said, "You don't want to get involved with a kid like this. Ten years old and he's already killed someone. Who's next?" He turned abruptly, stepped across the gangway, and the other two followed without looking back.

Once on the dock, Father Rolf moved toward the men with the fishing poles. None of them looked up. Faye held her breath while he asked, "Any of you boys seen a runaway?"

"Nope," one of them answered. The rest were silent. Then the solitary speaker added, "And we aren't boys."

Faye went below to prepare the engine. She could not risk another encounter with the authorities. "P.S.," she whispered, lifting her sleeping child to the top bunk, "you are very brave." To the boy hiding inside the bunk, she said, "When you hear the water moving against the hull, start counting to a thousand. Then come up on deck."

When Mark emerged from the hatch, the *Persephone* was well out of Belleville harbor.

"In the galley"—she pointed back down below—"there are potatoes to peel. They're in a bin under the sink."

Nervously he peeled, while Faye set sails and headed east along the coast. *He's just in time*, she thought to herself, having lost her crew. She'd picked up the occasional drifter, but no one had ever stayed for long. Now here was a fugitive boy—something she understood. As the sun sank into the lake and the potatoes boiled on the stove, she invited him on deck, offering him her jean jacket. It was much too big, and he seemed to swim in it, his dark head sprouting out of the collar. For a long time, neither of them spoke.

The wind in the rigging made a noise like a kettle coming to a partial boil, the little singing that means *not yet, not quite, hold on*. The helm felt heavy to Faye, as if the boat were resisting her. She found herself turning the wheel to counteract the boat's moves, steering like a beginner.

"I like it here." Mark waved at the lake around him. "No bugs," he said, as if pure enthusiasm for anything might mark him a coward. "It's been a long time since I spent a night without slapping."

"It's November," she said. "There are never bugs in November, even on land." Then she realized that he had just been trying to find a way to talk. She softened. "You don't live in a house?"

"Tepee," Mark said. "It's part of Rolf's plan. He gets money from the government. Jerk-offs. Excuse my French. Tells them he's using Indian ways. Vision quests, that bullshit. Excuse me again."

"Vision quests. What are those?"

Mark didn't answer. "The tepee's okay, but they put barbed wire around," he said, "even though most of us got no place to go if we decide to take off."

"Have no place," Faye said.

Mere poked her head up through the hatch. "I'm Mere."

"Mark. You're bare naked," Mark returned, causing Mere to sink back below.

"You take it," Faye said, moving the boy bodily to the big wooden helm and watching him take hold of it. "Good," she said, "watch the sails and keep them full. Watch the wind pennant. Is what those men said really true?" she asked, suddenly deciding to have it over with quickly.

"I went on a vision quest. Only, I don't know if I saw what I was supposed to." The boy ignored her question. Eventually Faye would learn that this was how Mark always replied, not as if a question was part of a dialogue between two people, but as if it existed outside of social convention as something that deserved long and serious contemplation. He only answered a good question when he was ready. For this reason, conversations with Mark never seemed to move forward. They looped back on themselves like a piece of macramé, something intricately knotted. Faye would come to the end of an evening spent talking to Mark, as he steered the boat, and find they were back at the beginning. She sometimes joked that the boat's keel carved the same circular trail in the water when he steered.

"Is what that priest said true?" she asked again.

"I don't even know what the old fart said."

"Watch your mouth. He said you killed someone." Faye couldn't believe her own tone. She was accusing a child who had come to her for help. But her own safety—and the safety of *her* child—came first. She heard Mark draw in his breath, then slowly exhale. He waited, and Faye turned her face to the bow, feeling the chilly fingers of the wind, not looking at the boy.

"Yeah."

Well, that's it, Faye thought, but it seemed to her there must be more to the story, and she found herself trying to blame his parents. The war. "Violence breeds violence," she said, but he was studying the dark sky, adjusting the big wheel. "You can't stay. I have a little girl."

"I'm good with kids. I took care of a lot of the little ones, the ones who tried to run. They didn't know any better."

"At the camp, there were kids younger than you?"

"The bigger kids sneaked through the fence. At night, they'd go to town to get pop and smokes, but they always came back." All this time the boy had been steering the boat, instinctively finding the groove where the sails and rudder balanced each other and the ship pointed close to the wind. He could barely see over the helm and the deckhouse, so he watched overhead, keeping the wind pennant parallel to the sail, as if he'd been doing it all his life.

Faye watched his face. It was ruddy, unwashed. His hair, badly cut. The teeth were chipped, crooked, but the mouth was wide and pleasant, the eyes, wonderfully direct.

"I got it," he said after a while.

"Looks like."

"How does a boat sail straight into the wind, anyway?" he asked.

When she didn't say anything, he said, "I killed my little brother, ma'am. But I can't go back." Her silence kept him talking. "It was Christmas and I was under the sink and I was talking to him on a walkie-talkie, giving him easy clues to find me, and after a while he wasn't answering, so I came out and he was playing with my new G.I. Joe gun. It was mine, not his, but I didn't care about that—it was just that he never asked—and he said, 'Hey, look, now it's mine,' or something like that, and I said no, but he was laughing, so I wanted to show him. I went into my dad's room, his closet, our dad, where the real gun was in case someone broke in or something, and I went to find my brother and show him the gun that was better than any stupid toy. I held it in my hand. It was heavy, and he made a jump to try and grab it. I tried to scare him, to make him back off. First he'd taken my gun, and now he was taking this gun that belonged to our dad and wasn't safe. So I said, 'Go away.' I meant to shoot up high but it was heavy—that part wasn't my fault."

The boy's voice was flat, running away like a dark wake. She would have to keep him.

"If you held the gun, it was your fault," she said, letting this first lesson sink in. Then, "You can stay, but you're not ever to tell Mere what you did."

✦

When Merril came into his basement, looking for Mere, two heads shot up from the other side of his sofa. "What the hell are you doing in my house?" he demanded of Mark.

Because he felt stupid half lying down, half sitting bolt upright, Mark stood up awkwardly. Merril was advancing, coming around the end of the sofa in steady strides. Unconsciously Mark clenched his fists.

"One of those kids who's always on the lookout for a fight," Merril said.

Mark glanced around. He couldn't find his voice. Mere was turning that bright red color that only she could turn. *Like something cooked*, Mark thought, only he wasn't thinking in words. He was thinking in pictures again, and feeling as if he were part of Mere, as if they shared the same skin, feeling her shame from the inside out.

Merril leaned over Mere and put his hand on her head. "Next time, you ask me before you invite over a boyfriend."

"But Mark's not . . ."

"Not what?" Merril was still resting his hand on her head. "He's some kind of runaway, I'd venture to say." He took his hand away.

"We weren't doing anything," Mark said, his voice finally coming to him.

It seemed to Mere that she didn't know how to behave in any world but her mother's, where lying beside Mark had been a comfort, not a shame.

"I'm going to talk to Mark now," Merril said gently. "You go upstairs."

Mere looked back as she left. Mark was trying not to look weak, straightening his back, planting his feet firmly on the floor.

Merril began, "Living together on a small boat must be fun, but that's all over with now."

"We never did anything."

"A boy like you living on a boat with a twelve-year-old girl and a crazy hippie."

His voice had shifted, Mark noticed, into a darker register. He was circling Mark, not even looking at him.

"So who are you? What are you hiding from?"

"Do you see me hiding?"

"That's Faye's thing. For her, fugitives are a big turn-on. What from?" Merril pushed on. "Would you be up here from the States? No, you're too young. What'd you do—crack a vending machine, steal the quarters?"

Mark was quiet but Merril persisted. "Must have been something bad," he said, "to keep you on the lake . . . for how long? What if I call the police?"

Mark said, "I'm old enough to decide where to live."

Merril was pursing his lips. "Legal age?"

"I'm sixteen."

"Sixteen. No wonder you're horny."

Mark moved around the room, picking up his jacket, the slip of paper with Merril's address.

"Watch what you take," Merril said with a hint of threat

in his voice. "You aren't on a boat at the moment and you can't just sail away."

Mark only wanted this conversation to end. "Right."

Merril picked up an empty pack of cigarettes and tossed them at the boy. "Take your trash and go out the back way."

Mark stood on the street in front of Merril's house, furious and afraid. Police. His nightmare. And if they followed him to Faye? Always he had protected her from that. He rubbed his chapped hands over his face and through his hair. The encounter had shaken him, and he took a jab with his boot at a pile of frozen leaves. The prick knew the boat—he'd been down there yesterday—and he would do what he'd threatened, send the cops. So the worst thing Mark could do would be to go back. Faye had told him to bring Mere home, but that was impossible now.

He began to run, hard and fast, the cold air stinging his lungs and throat. He ran along the frozen sidewalks, his arms flapping by his sides, cold sweat on his forehead. *Put some distance between yourself and that house. That prick. Some distance between yourself and Mere.* With this thought he stopped, jamming his hands in his back pockets. Great puffs of air issued from his mouth.

Stay out of the light. Keep in the shadows.

He was not the one to help Faye. There was an ache in his heart that allowed him sometimes to convince himself that he was like others, that he deserved the company of someone as high-minded as Faye. But he did not.

Panting, bent over now, he felt the acid taste of vomit in his throat.

On the vision quest, he'd proved once and for all what he was made of: he'd tried, he had willed himself to see something, anything, to hear a message, but nothing had come to him. No vision, no light or wisdom, just a terrible emptiness, an understanding that he amounted to nothing. A hole. A zero. The bit of chocolate on his mouth—a stain. His father's handkerchief—another kindness, like Faye's, that he did not deserve. His brother spinning the little wheel of the car. His brother's laugh. Every time he tried to change, the emptiness inside him spread. Father Rolf had said, "You're a black one" after Mark had snuck out to buy cigarettes. And Rolf was right. But he would not go back to those fences, the punishment. With that thought, he began again to run.

✦

Mere lay in her bed with Rogue at her feet. *Everything*, she told herself, *is straight here. Except me*. All day, she'd felt that it was too much for her, everything being fixed in its place, everything still. And then the scene with Mark and her father had upset everything. When she was little, she had looked out the portholes and sometimes caught a glimpse of a passing freighter. The ships moved by so fast that she couldn't tell whether they were going to smash into the *Persephone*, and once she'd told Faye that she had to be on deck to watch out in case a big boat came straight at them. "Moving is a comfort," Faye had said then. "If you watch another boat and it stays in one place, that's when you should be afraid. That means collision course."

After that, Mere knew what to watch out for. Stillness. But even then she'd begun dreaming of a shipwreck, a rock that would run the *Persephone* aground. In some of her dreams, she climbed out of the boat and walked across dry land. She was afraid at first, in the dreams, but she did not turn back.

Now, stowed inside her father's house where nothing moved, she pulled the blankets close and tried not to think about how all the houses on the street were unmoving. *It's because I don't have the clock. I can't touch it.* The door opened, and a long square of light stretched across the floor.

"I came in to say goodnight." Merril sounded tired.

"Ellie tucked me in," said Mere, sliding over and making room for him on the bed. She smells better than anyone, Mere wanted to say, to diffuse the shame she still felt about what had happened with Mark. But she only managed to lie still.

"Rogue keeping your feet warm?"

She wanted to explain about Mark and how they loved each other, but not the way Merril had made it sound. She wanted to explain how everything on land seemed as if it might suddenly smash together. But she was afraid that he might feel hurt, and knew he would probably try to talk her out of such a strange idea anyway. "What's the best thing that ever happened to you?" she asked, hoping he would tell her his version of her birth.

But he was lost in his own thoughts. The meeting with

Gil had unsettled him, shaken his confidence in his half-formed plan. He'd never been a planner. An initiator, maybe. What was his next step? Comfort the child, talk for a little while. What had she asked? He said, "For a guy, I guess nothing's ever quite as good as when you're young." He put his hand on the top of her head, the way he had before and said, "Playing football. I was just like your friend Mark, sixteen. A kid. Hitting everything hard, full concentration. Football. I'm not talking about war. A gun doesn't make you something—you don't even see what you're hitting. As we used to say about the war, it takes guts to go, but it takes balls to say no."

She thought, *What's wrong with him*? At the same time, she wanted to keep her father talking to keep him close, as if his words or physical presence could make up for her growing awareness that he had not thought much about her in all these years. He had not been on land wishing for some shipwreck to bring him his daughter. But now, for some reason, he wanted her. That was something.

"Where'd you grow up?" she asked.

"Pennsylvania," he said. "Let's leave it at that."

"How come? You didn't like it there?"

"I got tired of running to the corner store to buy my mother cigarettes and a beer."

"Where was your dad?" she asked, thinking maybe they had something in common.

"Good question."

Mere tried to relax. She said, "Chicago is where you and Faye started me."

"Is that what she told you?"

Mere tried to sit up. She didn't feel comfortable lying

down next to him, but he had hold of her arm. "She was really young then," Mere said thoughtfully. "But you were already older."

"Twenty-five," Merril said, suddenly wanting her to understand. "That's young, kiddo. And I was full of action. Wild. Revolutionary stunts. I was going to change the government and everything else in the process." He laughed in a strained way. "Can you believe it of this mild-mannered guy?" As he said it, he realized that he liked having the child in his house because he wasn't young anymore and she gave him something to show for all the years he'd been living this uprooted life. Something besides Ellie and the cars and the macaws. Something that would react to him, look up to him, something that was a someone. Unconditional.

The light through the bedroom door was striped with the shadow of the banister, like the shadow from a cage or the shadow cast on the water by the boards of a floating dock. She had been listening carefully to his silence, and now she looked up at his face. "Why were you trying to change everything?"

"It's a long story. You must have heard it all before."

The softness of his voice does not match the rest of him, Mere thought. "I don't talk to grown-ups."

"Don't you talk to your mother?"

"Sure. But she doesn't remember much about all that." Mere did not want to be questioned about her mother. She wanted to know about the father she had lost. But Merril was remembering the thrill of running through the streets of Chicago with a clock wired to dynamite.

He looked down now at the child he had made. Out of

thin air. Out of his rage. And for a moment, he remembered the shelter of her mother's body. Merril stood up then, but reached out to touch Mere once again. "Actually, not sixteen," he said, withdrawing his hand. "Maybe that wasn't the best time. The best was a few years later."

But Mere had drifted into her own thoughts. *If my mother comes to his house, then I will know she thinks I am worth more than her ideas.*

A RAGGED COURSE

Faye stepped off the ferry at the hour when the islands were a thin tiara of light across the water, when they appeared to be quite remote. More than a mile of dark water separated her from the ship. Mark hadn't come back. Everything on the city side, along the shore, was new and raw or old and broken down, grain elevators rising beside deep holes lined with cement blocks and steel reinforcing rods and illuminated by construction lights. In front of one of these foundations, she stopped and looked down. *It was just such a rod.* She felt the surprise of tears mixed with great, patient flakes of snow. The flakes were drifting down from the lowering sky while in front of her was a vast hole full of blood-colored water out of which sprang the implements of steel that could hold up a tower or stop time.

A wind had come up, and she turned back to her walking, moving slowly through soggy trash, dog shit, and mud. Wishing she had good boots, and wondering what shoes Mere had been wearing when she left. What were her daughter's resources and how were they matched against Merril's? The sidewalk was blocked at another site where the terminal building was being reconstructed, so she crossed the street and walked north under an overpass that spanned a great distance. Where was she going? Against the darkness, she saw her reflection in the glass wall of an office tower. *This isn't so different from the lake*, she thought, and the thought comforted her; for a minute she couldn't remember why she had stayed away from land so long. It was probably easier to lose yourself in a city, she realized, noticing a burned-out building, boarded up. Across the door someone had painted the word VIRUS. The windows were broken and a red banner hung from one of them with a message on it, but the letters were from an unrecognizable alphabet. They were pieces of a revolution Faye did not understand, although she might have, she thought, if she'd gone underground in the city. Might have raised Mere somehow in a house with a yard. Might have sent her to school . . . Mere had seen all of this now. Mere knew what she'd missed. Why had she ever let her daughter escape?

Even at night, here on land, there were shops open with lights and silver counters. But Faye did not enter them. Restaurants and bars lined the sidewalks. A car sat stalled on the street. Stranded. Beached. Its hood open, as if the machines of the city were dying. And on a dark corner, a man waited silent and alone, gesturing. Faye tried to memorize the faces of the other pedestrians, in case it came to that, then tried not to think about anything but the present action. But she could not help staring at the man. What was he doing? What were his mittened hands so busy saying? She saw him walk a few paces, then return to stand in the same place, gesturing with palms up, as if explaining something complex to someone else. *There is more than enough dynamite.* The man turned again, slowly, and walked to the end of the block, where he stood quietly absorbed in his interior debate. *Like me*, she thought, and found herself wondering whether she was the only one of the old collective still living out of sight, and if so, how would she know? They had talked about it at the time. About having contacts above ground so you wouldn't go crazy. So you would have some idea of yourself. But she had lost those contacts long ago when Merril and Gil had departed. In the end, her only connection had been Gil's envelope of cash the dock master handed her when she arrived in Toronto. Twice a year. That envelope, her thin line to the world, to Liza Greene, to her past. For a while, Gil had stepped into the breach Merril had made with his leaving. For a while, he had made it possible to go on. Caring for Mere during the afternoon hours, when Faye took the helm, he managed the child with miraculous patience and tirelessness. For a few months of that time, the commotion within Faye seemed to subside, and the boat slipped back and forth between the shores of New York and Ontario entirely unnoticed, carrying its refugees.

Joe Nakayama was the last fugitive Gil helped her to save. Joe's father had heard about their mission in a run-down bar on the Genesee River. Just turned eighteen, Joe was scheduled to report the following week, but Joe's father went home, told Joe to pack, and drove him down to the harbor himself, without a word to the mother of his son. For a long time, Joe's father stood with his hat in hand and watched his son disappear. Two days later, when they reached Kingston and the immigration officer stamped Joe's landing papers, Faye went to the galley to pack a lunch for him. She could hear him on the other side of the hatch, taking his clothes out of a locker by his bunk. Gil was with him, and she could hear him asking Joe, in hushed conversation, to stay aboard for a few more weeks until things settled down, "until I can get word to you, and some money for Faye."

Faye interrupted Gil. "So you're leaving me too."

"It takes more than baby quilts to survive," Gil said. He nodded toward Joe. "There will be boys to crew. I can do more for you on shore."

Now she was standing in the snow, staring at a wild man in a long coat and woolen cap. It seemed to her that when the hard snows came, when the wind struck with its winter force, this man in his solitude would still be standing or wandering this street, gesturing, for he had turned again and come back to his corner, where he stood in the cold dark with his mittened palms up, taking no notice of anything around him. What was his argument? *Blow up the statue.* The one that had withstood the grueling heat of countless summers, rains of countless storms, sleet and wind of countless winters in order to remember a policeman, dead in a riot. *Sacrifice the statue. It'll be prophetic.* His mittened palms upturned, the wild man considered only the present action. *Connect the wire to the blasting cap. Be careful when you thread the clock. Concentrate on the work of your hands. The dynamite is threaded last. Six sticks. Then the girl with long brown hair and a thin face will put it in a cardboard box. You'll let her risk this much. Then take it yourself, at midnight. After you've strapped it to the statue, go back to the boat. But not in a straight line. A ragged course is the idea. Set a ragged course.*

The gears of another city were turning. She understood that whatever was happening to her was part of the machine they'd set in motion thirteen years before. She felt the stiffness of Gil's cash in the pocket of her jeans. *Gil.* His name would be in the phone book.

One ring, and then the familiar voice. "Hello?"

"It's Faye." She heard a click on the line and a woman's voice.

"Hello?"

"I got it," Gil said. After the clatter of the woman hanging up, he spoke quickly. "Don't say where you are."

Her heart beat faster, faster.

"He's making some kind of deal."

She spit out, "He's got Mere."

"I know." Faye was waiting for the old familiarity, a softness in his voice. But he was all business. "You've got to say goodbye to your Persephone now."

"I have." Mere was with Merril. "Tell me where he lives."

"No. Impossible. You can't take that risk."

She hung up the phone and stood in the glass booth staring at it. She touched the metal cord for a second, then slid down the inside of the phone booth onto her haunches, burying her face in her hands.

A tall woman, wearing fur that reached nearly to her ankles, looked surprised when Faye asked her to decipher the address in the phone book. "I'm just visiting," Faye explained, nervous. The woman knew the street, knew the neighborhood. "Subway's the quickest." Her hands, heavy with gold, pointed to stairs that led underground.

Faye realized that, except for hasty trips to her parents' dank basement when she was a child, she'd never been underground in her life. She had floated, trying to make no mark. Now she put one foot exactly in front of the other, as if to cover her own tracks. Step by step, without turning back, down under King Street. The claustrophobia of the subway rushed up at her.

At the foot of the stairs, a small kiosk with magazines, newspapers, and candy bars. She hovered at its rim, but could not decide what she wanted. A little present for Mere, a piece of licorice. Behind the magazine stand, she saw a corridor full of light. There were shops with dresses in the windows. A whole world underground, electrified and intense. She began to walk toward the shops and saw in a window a basket full of puppies in a heaped, sleepy pile. Now she thought of the time the collective had first crept down to the harbor to her rocking boat. She liked the feel of sleeping bodies, especially when she was awake herself. Moving quietly in the darkness to tend to the engine, to prime the water pump, to store leftover food and visit the head by herself. A sensation of peace and power, as if she were truly a guardian in charge of a litter of lives. Later, she had loved the hours when the children were asleep. Mark in his bunk; Mere curled in hers, the *Persephone* rocking and sighing, sometimes sailing on a single sail so she could maneuver the ship herself, sometimes anchored for the night. It seemed now that years had gone by like that, her best hours solitary except for the slumbering sound of human animals.

And last night? Where had Mere slept?

In the corridor, mirrored pillars multiplied the bodies that walked past, an endless stream of men and women and small children in strollers.

There were places to drink flavored tea or buy tobacco. She saw something called a food court with counters circling it. Each counter served a different kind of food: Chinese, Italian, Mexican, even Vietnamese. *Self-government!* Faye wondered what people in Vietnam ate. She wondered why she had been sailing between two countries for years, proud of the fact that she belonged to neither of them. She had no passport. Her only identification papers were counterfeit. She'd torn up flags and made them into quilts. She'd taught the children to embroider over the ensigns of ships. She had been a fool. All this time moving on the movable substance of water, and the world had been moving even faster, as if there were no borders or nations, just a mass of humanity craving and providing. As if all the flavors had run together and every taste in the world could be had for a dollar or a dime. Saigon. Hanoi. That tunnel in between.

"Which way is the cleaner's?"

"Sorry," she whispered.

"You all right?" *Po' gal.*

She broke into a sweat. "I'm trying to find my daughter." But she stopped, having given too much away.

"Report it! If she's missing, report it, dear. Terrible things can happen in the city."

People in front of her and behind her, so many people. Then the great train that roared into the tunnel and stopped her heart. The crowd coming out of the subway car pushed her back, and she stumbled and stood clinging to a pillar. When the next train came in, she heard herself scream with the brakes. She entered with people who carried her along, riding a current; she found a seat, and the train started with a jolt. There was a flash, then the darkness. Faye held her breath. Hands gripping metal, she shut her eyes. The train shrieked and screamed. It rumbled into a platform bright with artificial light, slowed, and opened its doors, although no one got off or on, then lurched again into the night. Faye began to think of moving between night and day in a matter of seconds, of time sped up, of each stop as another part of the cycle of her life with nothing to mark the years but light—dark—light. Did people who were dying really see their whole lives flash in front of their eyes? She had stood over someone dying, she had seen his eyes. But had he seen her or had he been looking at something inside?

The dark ride would go on and on under the city. The city too would go on and on forever overhead. Here, in the dark underworld of pipes and valves and tunnels and sewers, of people rushing in and out of holes, of rats and viruses and corners with occupied sleeping bags, she felt that she had come to a place where it was possible, at last, to relive any moment in her life. She could watch her father sitting beside her as she steered the *Persephone*. His cap low over his ears, he smoked a cigarette, telling her to keep her eyes on the horizon. Never look back. Her father, sitting on a seat across from her, barking to someone on deck. Who was it, in blue high heels with silver buckles? She could see her mother folded neatly in a coffin unmourned, wearing a flowered dress. Her mother had been generous, Faye could see that now too. Her mother had wanted the best for Faye, knitting patience and solitude around her small fragility.

Faye had left her mother behind. As if living on a boat had been the right thing to do.

She saw that, like Mere, she was a runaway child. And was it possible to go forward and forward, without water or air or light, to explain this to her daughter?

Merril walked past the room where Ellie slept, past the bedroom where he had said goodnight to Mere, along the open hallway, and into his office. From the drawer of his desk, he took the gun, weighing it in his hand as if it would provide some kind of confidence. They had a van parked in the alley. He sat back in his chair, propped his feet up on the crowded desk, and considered his words. Carefully. They'd put the pin in the map. They were going to get Faye one way or the other. Making a deal meant he would be there to take care of the child. His child. Who was going to turn his life around.

Thinking of her under his roof, he tucked the gun into his waist and lifted the phone, dialing the number of a pizza delivery place. "I want to order a large, with anchovies." He heard the line clicking and said, "I know you're sitting out there listening. Okay, I'm willing to talk. Except that I have my daughter now and I'm keeping her, that's part of the deal." He thought he sounded reasonably calm, calmer than he felt. "I'll tell you where her mother is, but I want all charges against me dropped and no news about this to reach my investors or employees." Now he pushed his voice down to a lower pitch. "When you've got that written down, you can walk it over to my front door and we can get this rolling." He dropped the phone in its cradle and turned to find Mere in the doorway. How long had she been standing there?

"I want to go back to my boat."

"That's not possible." Merril got up smoothly and made his way to her. Hand on her back, he tried to force her into the hall. When she resisted, he swung his arm around her and lifted, carrying her down the hall to her room, where he dropped her on the bed. "Try not to think," he said.

He walked out of the room and shut the door, turning the old-fashioned key in the lock.

Mark could see no sign of movement in Merril's house. He stood in the same spot on the street he'd run from earlier, the sting of his humiliating encounter with Merril still on his skin. He had run a few blocks, and then he had turned and found his way back. Faye believed in him. She was alone in the world in this belief, which made going back to reform school or even jail almost insignificant. He would do as he had promised and bring Mere back to her.

There was a light on upstairs close to the middle, about where Mere had slept the night before. He'd seen the room. Getting up to it from the outside would be easy. It was after nine o'clock now. Mere might even be asleep. Mark found a water spout that was well hooked to the corner of the house and led to an overhang. Hand over hand, with his feet against the wall, he shimmied up, his shirt and jacket bunching over his belly. He scrambled onto a shingled ledge, then over to the lit window that sat under a small gabled roof. Pressing his face against the glass, Mark saw a picture of a man playing a guitar and beneath that the big bed with a thick blue blanket. Curled in a ball on the blanket lay Mere. It looked to him as if she was crying.

On the first knock, Mere started. The two children had lived so long together, and in such close quarters, that they were accustomed to tapping and whispering. They were used to hand signals and covert glances. They were accomplished conspirators. Now Mere reached across the bed to the window and yanked on the latch. *It's stuck*, she mouthed.

He shrugged and tried to force the window. When it held, he raised his dark eyebrows and pointed at her bedroom door. But Mere shook her head. *Locked*, she mouthed again.

They looked at each other for a moment through the glass, then Mark made an X across his chest with his finger, promising to get her out.

He slouched along the ledge to the water pipe, which now looked precarious, but he shimmied down, landing on the ground with a *thud*. He stood in the dark garden, catching his breath.

At Rosedale station, just as she had been told, Faye stepped off the train and stumbled up cold, wet stairs, telling herself to breathe again and finding it strange that so much snow had fallen on the streets. As if she had been riding the underground train for a season. She looked up, and the snow fell into her eyes. Then she saw the moon, her blind friend, pale in the sky.

"Where's Cluny Drive?" she demanded of a passerby.

A hand took her elbow. "Follow that row of trees. You'll see the street sign. Turn right."

The wind had picked up. Overhead telephone wires swung and in the branches whatever birds there were braced themselves against the gusts. Snow swirled around dizzily. Bare trees heaved and snapped overhead, like the clutching hands of the drowned. At the first corner, Faye saw the street sign and turned onto a sidewalk that sloped down a hill.

Mere had spent a night on dry, unheaving land in one of these houses, one of these rooms looking out on this man-created world. She'd slept not on a bunk that was hers and hers alone, but on a bed made for anyone, bought from a store. Did it have a bedspread of roses or lace? *Do not fall in love with frilly curtains, with oven mitts in the shape of animals, with Chinese powder boxes.*

Do not step on a crack.

Following the bitter smell of car exhaust that came on the wind, Faye made her way slowly, finding it hard to discern in the dark the houses set behind fences and tall shrubs. The snow had begun to swirl into blinding clouds, and she paused long enough to catch her breath and gather herself into firmness. Finally she was calm, walking the path she had set out for herself so long ago. *I might have done it all differently.* Over the years, she had remembered more details. Images had become sharper; each moment separate and distinct, as if all the time she'd been underground she had also been unwinding and rewinding those moments, playing them across her mind in order to understand. *We began to arrive in Chicago on the fifth. And on October sixth he blew up the statue. There was more than enough dynamite.*

Standing there on the sidewalk, Faye knew that she could tell Mere the story.

If Mere understood, the past might seem less potent. She might even make a different life for her child. She saw the brass numbers on the large black mailbox, turned in to the driveway, and caught a quick glimpse of a small head visible for an instant at a second-floor window. She held her breath as a shade was pulled against the moon-heavy night, and once again she felt her child sinking into a deep, black lake. Out of reach. Out of sight.

"I'm telling you, man, it went off without a hitch. Nobody got hurt. It was beautiful. More than enough dynamite. Six sticks." Talking. Talking. All day they had been pacing, talking, getting ready, arranging the equipment they would carry. For attack. For defense. All day their voices, questions, their rage. "Thousands. That's what they expect."

They carried their helmets, flashlights, spray cans, electrical tape, a length of rope. They had smoked together. They were coiled. *Steel yourselves!* Running up the dock with shouts and whoops, they hit the long swath of green that bound the shore of the lake to the city. "Slow down. Take it easy now. And keep eyes in the back of your head. Be ready for any surprise."

When they got deeper in, they began skirting main thoroughfares, ducking into alleys that smelled of trash and human piss.

There would be uniforms posted around the park, circling like dogs, like jackals, with their sprays and guns and heavy plastic shields. *Ready to debate! Steel yourselves!* There was fire up ahead. They could feel its smoke around them, could smell its sweet sting in the air, a sting made of leaves and wood. "Fire! This is it!"

Around the last corner, a phalanx of plastic shields, billy clubs, a sea of dark uniforms and faces that glared from under helmets. *They hate us, as if we're different.* Black leather holsters, shiny black boots.

In an alley, she opened a jar, swept her finger through the pitch, and turned to Ahab, wiping it across his face, drawing a mustache over his mouth. "Ah, gee," he protested, with a laugh. Carefully then, she covered everything but his eyes. Now they would blend into the soon-coming dark.

More of them. Greased faces, round eyes, helmets—they were disappearing into a giant mass; they had lost themselves. Around them were hundreds of others. How many? So many people milling and shouting instructions to each other, handing out wooden clubs and steel rods. She reached out for one as she walked into the park.

Someone in camouflage with a bullhorn exhorted the

assembled crowd. "You are here tonight because you are the only true revolutionaries in America to put your lives on the line! We come together as a non-racist community of true revolutionaries!" A pause. "Brothers! You are here to put your only lives on the line!" Or did he say, *only your lives?*

Her eyes burned. Were they using tear gas? "Make them show their fascist face!" she cried out, hearing someone beside her shout, "Marion Delgado," the code word meant to spring them into action.

A pressure, a crush of flesh pushing, uniforms shouting. Ahab's hand tighter and tighter on hers. Her chest, compressed, hurting. She had to remind herself to breathe. Like fire, the crowd rolled and expanded to the edge of the park. Someone had a dog in his arms. A bandana on a man's head, not a helmet. She saw a face covered in tears. Someone vomiting. A mob of fury, they expanded like another kind of element, molten, into the street. Swinging clubs and rods and shouting, they streamed up the nameless street to a corner where buildings closed tight against the sea of arms and legs.

Cop cars, alive with lights and sirens, roared into the alleys and streets. The one with the bandana on his head was thrown across a hood, face and body beaten. The crash of glass. Then smashing and chanting. She wanted to take off her helmet—it was heavy, too big, her head kept banging against the sides—but a woman with blood dripping from her forehead crumpled. *Keep the helmet.* "Stay close!" "Slow down!" "Kill the pigs!" "They're all over us!" "Hit the bank first!"

She rushed at the bank, raising the rod and throwing her weight behind a swing. She felt the thrill of her effort multiply as others followed. "Kill the banks!"

The shriek of alarms.

Where glass had been, an open space. Bodies poured through it. Rioters smashed at lamps, desks, countertops. A flag hung from the ceiling. She vaulted up onto the counter and tore it down. From above, she could see two cops leap through the shattered glass. Clubs raised, they swung on the surging crowd.

She is aware of Ahab across the room, mid-motion, ripping a phone cord from the wall, sees him pause, drop the phone, pick up a metal chair, and rush at one of the uniforms.

She hears Ahab's roar above everything as he brings the chair down across the man's back.

Another one pulls a gun from his holster. Holding it stiffly, he takes careful aim.

This trinity: the wounded man, the man with the gun, and Ahab.

Outside, the sky, perfect, a blue that lights the trio as in a still life.

"Stand down," the one with the gun yells.

The wounded one struggles to his feet.

"Stand down!"

And Ahab wheels around, seeing the gun, raising his hands as if to grab at the barrel.

He is going to kill Ahab.

Dark faces and blue sky beyond the broken glass. Someone smiles idiotically, showing white teeth, but nothing else moves and there is no sound. She is deafened by rage, lifting the steel in both hands, holding it straight, the blue sky, the rod in her hands making an arc, striking the neck and shoulders of the man with the gun. *Yes.* She feels flesh and bone as he collapses, but not before she hears the crack of gunfire, sees the flare at the gun's tip, as if it is a cartoon pistol.

Ahab grabs at his shoulder.

Then she is howling. Leaping from the counter onto Ahab, who is on the floor.

Hands that have dropped the gun, black hands, grab uselessly at the air.

"STOP NOW! They shot Ahab!" Who? "Shut up. Run!" Gil grabs her. Gil? Rushes to them, urging them up.

Out of the building now, into the street, between struggling bodies. Someone is pushing a shirt at Ahab's shoulder. "I'm bleeding!"

"You're not. You're fine."

The man lying in the bank. Flesh broken open. She is holding on to Ahab, dragging.

What happens next she remembers in fits and starts—the long, crazed run to the boat, taking a ragged course, Ahab bleeding and crying, holding the shirt, now clotted with blood. It seems too difficult to remember a time before the man lay on the floor. *My hand's ringing*, she thinks, feeling pain in her fingers and wrists. And someone has started the engines. "He needs a doctor!" Someone says, *Canada.*

She is alone in the night shadow of Merril's driveway, a hundred paces from his gate. She takes them softly, raising her eyes to the darkened window. To lift the child one last time from her sleep. To move on. Because only moving is safe. Stealing into the blackness of the garden, she picks up a fallen pear. Mere sleeps in a room beside a tree surrounded by the desiccated garden of autumn. *The man I killed was also someone's child.*

And what is left? What we have is not nothing (her mother's nursery wisdom): what we have is just this. A house behind a hedge. A child inside. A glass door that is dark, but perhaps unlocked. "Purpose," she says under her breath, noticing a rustle of leaves, the whine of a dog, the street light dappling the hedge, and somewhere a car engine running softly. The glass door reflects nothing, but her feet find the steps.

A car pulls into the driveway and the headlights freeze Faye in place. *I need to hold my child.* But a man climbs out of the driver's side, and it's as if she is still standing on the stern, watching Mere drop into the lake. The man is running into the yard, up the steps, yanking her arm. "Faye." She recognizes his face. Softer, his hair gray at the temples, but a face of memory. "Let's go." He drags her by the arm back down the steps. This man who, if he takes her now, will be harboring a fugitive.

"No, Gil." She plants her feet firmly in wet grass.

"This is madness."

But Mere is inside. Mere. Her only life. "No." The dog begins to bark. Faye and Gil are locked in a tug-of-war as the glass door slides along its track and a boy—it must be

Mark—emerges into the garden, whispering, "Hurry up, and watch out." Then slips into the dark.

"Mere," Faye chokes out. Because it's true. Mere has emerged into the cold garden.

"Mama." Mere leaps at her mother, and Faye takes her daughter into her arms, pressing the perfect so-loved head against her breast and sobbing. Now they both cry, and it is Gil who says, "Come on," shoving mother and daughter toward his waiting car.

But Merril has stepped out of the glass doors, the dog by his side, as a van pulls in behind Gil's car, and two men get out of it, moving into the yard.

Then Mere howls.

It is a howl that understands what is lost, and it rides on the wind and snow, for winter has arrived.

But the mother does not think of that. She thinks only of the heat and desire and love that brought them to this season.

ACKNOWLEDGMENTS

Thanks and love to Michael Ondaatje and Douglas Fudge, who endured the vagaries of this project, providing support and merciless encouragement and reading numerous drafts.

Our thanks to Iris Tupholme, who took on the necessary role of editor and referee with humor, grace, and wisdom. To Michael Redhill, our careful, diligent reader. To Jan Whitford, who saw this through to the end, and Jackie Kaiser, who carries it forward. To Nicole Langlois, for her care and patience with the manuscript. To Gloria Bishop, Gillian Deacon, Quintin Ondaatje, Miranda Pearson, Constance Rooke, and David Young for their insights. To Adrienne, who began the conversation. To Gregor and Beatrice von Rezzori, for the gracious gift of their tower at Santa Magdalena. To Yvonne Hunter, for her work on behalf of the book. To the Banff Centre for the Arts Studio Program, and Cassandra Pybus, who provided company and gin. To Toronto Brigantine for inspiration and experience. To Kristin, who is part of this too.